HOW I

WONDER

WHAT

YOU ARE

HOW I WONDER WHAT YOU ARE

L. M. Lynch

ALFRED A. KNOPF
NEW YORK

THIS IS A BORZOI BOOK PUBLISHED BY ALFRED A. KNOPF

Text copyright © 2001 by L. M. Lynch
Jacket illustration © 2001 by Robert Hunt

Library of Congress Cataloging-in-Publication Data
Lynch, L. M.
How I wonder what you are / L. M. Lynch.
p. cm.
Summary: Sixth grader Laurel finds herself increasingly preoccupied with her younger
sister's strange behavior, the unusual boy who has appeared in her neighborhood and
class at school, and the disappearance of the wonderful climbing tree that may have
been cut down by his family.
ISBN 0-375-80663-6 (trade) — ISBN 0-375-90663-0 (lib. bdg.)
[1.Sisters—Fiction. 2. Schools—Fiction. 3. Trees—Fiction.] I. Title.
PZ7.L97976 Ho   2001
[Fic]—dc21   00-049766

Printed in the United States of America
August 2001
10 9 8 7 6 5 4 3 2 1
First Edition

For Peter Lloyd-Davies: technical adviser, husband, and best friend

chapter 1

Pools of sweat are forming between Laurel's skin and the leather armchair—that's how hot it is. Outside has got to feel cooler than this sweatbox. So why can't she seem to budge from the chair? *Give me strength,* Laurel thinks in a kind of prayer. *Better yet, give me air-conditioning.*

Laurel's mom, meanwhile, keeps shouting things from some other room. "Answer me, Jeanie!" she is shouting. But Laurel's younger sister, Jeanie, stretched out on the floor near Laurel, isn't answering. She's probably watching the TV inside her head. Jeanie claims she gets over a hundred channels.

A scream is building inside Laurel like steam in a kettle. She's tired of the summer heat. Tired of her mother's shouting. And she's incredibly tired of a sister who watches an inner television.

Laurel finally manages to pry herself out of the sticky armchair. She squats down next to Jeanie and pokes her sister's shoulder.

"Why won't you answer Mom?" Laurel says it through her teeth. Maybe if she clenches her teeth hard enough, she won't actually start screaming.

"Shush! There's something on the Balloon Channel right

now," Jeanie whispers. "It's a special. About the Balloon Planet."

The Balloon Planet, Laurel silently repeats. *Is that where balloons go when they disappear into the sky?* An image of the planet starts taking shape in her mind. Then she catches herself. *Oh man,* she thinks. *My little sister is going to turn me into a nutcase.* She jumps up and heads for the door.

"I'm taking a walk on the trail," she calls. "I've got to get out of here."

Mrs. Shade sticks her head around the corner. She has a crazed-looking, stretched-elastic grin. "Can I come, too? Please?" she says. It's her little way of joking.

Seeing the cut-down tree for the first time was confusing. One minute it was just a walk down the trail on a hot day, cicadas buzzing frantically, air smelling like baked grass. Then something about the light seemed funny. Then all the trees started to look like trees Laurel had never seen before—and why was that little white-shingled house standing out for the first time?

Only then did Laurel see the tree—actually, she saw the empty space where the tree used to be.

The tree that was gone was the best-known tree in Chestnut Knoll, the one the kids called the "climbing tree." Laurel's father said it was actually a cork tree, maybe some dwarf species, because the tree wasn't very big but the bark looked old.

Laurel looked at the stump. It was a low, flat disk, mostly dark brown, with light rings near the edges. It had a raw look that made her cringe.

A lurching, sickened feeling was spreading through her. The climbing tree couldn't be gone. It *could not just be gone* like this. It was part of her life, part of growing up in Chestnut Knoll. They might as well have taken a wrecking ball to her bedroom. Or bull-dozed Tuckerman School. The kids should have been told. They should have been asked. This was not real, not possible.

Laurel closed her eyes. Maybe if she counted to ten, when she opened her eyes again the tree would be there. She began counting, eyes squeezed shut. But they fluttered open when a voice near her ear said, "Something the matter with you?"

A boy with freckles and a backward baseball cap stood straddling a mountain bike. He grinned at Laurel. His front teeth were huge and gray.

He waggled his thumb in the direction of the disk that had been the climbing tree. "Pretty amazing, huh?" He made it sound like he'd just heard a good joke.

"It's horrible. It's sickening. What happened?"

"Don't ask me," the boy said. "Some guy cut it down."

Laurel could hardly imagine a more horrific deed. They were in a nature preserve! "Who could do a thing like that?"

"Some guy," the boy repeated.

"What do you mean, *some guy*?"

But the boy seemed suddenly to lose interest in the climbing-tree discussion. Without another word, he lifted his bike and turned his back on Laurel.

"What *guy*?" Laurel practically shrieked. She now despised this boy and all his freckles.

"Some new guy," he said sullenly. And then, just before he pedaled away: "Holyfield. Holyfield, someone said."

Holyfield. The name gave her goose bumps, even in the afternoon heat.

As she pushed through the back door, Laurel nearly collided with her father. Amazing—he was actually home for dinner!

He made a formal declaration once they'd sat down to eat: "I have finished!" Laurel's dad was a biology professor, and he was finally done with all the last-minute double-checking for the textbook he'd written. The publication deadline had been ruining dinners for quite a while now, so there was a feeling of excitement at the table. Everyone was laughing and talking, sometimes all at once. The Shades were leaving for vacation in two days, but tonight it felt as if vacation had already started.

It's kind of strange, Laurel thought. Everything about her dad seemed gentle and soft. Soft reddish blond beard and hair and eyebrows. Soft shirts. Even his ears had a particular softness, a peachy-velvety look. He was actually very quiet. But when he wasn't around, things felt off.

Good spirits were really pouring out of him right now. His book was finally finished. He was telling them about how a computer crash in the final hours had nearly wiped out all his data, managing to make it sound almost funny. "It's actually good when the whole system crashes." He paused. He stroked his beard reflectively. "It helps you realize there's a problem."

His story was cut off by an abrupt shriek.

"Pause the meal!" Jeanie was shouting. As she jumped up, the table lurched. Then she was gone.

Laurel was irritated. "Why do you let her leave the table like that? Aren't we supposed to ask to be excused?"

Laurel knew that her mother believed in ignoring Jeanie's bad behavior whenever possible, rather than "rewarding" it with attention. But Laurel herself had doubts about this child-rearing philosophy. Major doubts. And funny how it had never been applied to *her.*

In fact, the more she thought about it, the more unfair it all seemed. Why should Jeanie be allowed to just cruise around under her own rules? She was seven years old, after all, not some baby.

And why wasn't anybody even bothering to answer Laurel now?

"Could someone please answer me?" Laurel practically hissed. Her father gave her a puzzled look. Her mother just sighed.

Okay. Fine. *Don't* answer. Honestly, Jeanie could probably stand up on the table and… and do a rabid chicken imitation, and her parents would just smile and say, "Oh, Jeanie."

When Jeanie returned to the table, she plopped down hard into her chair. "I had to check the channel guide for my television," she announced. Then she hunched low, head down, and watched her fingers fight with one another.

"By the way, Jeanie," Laurel said, "you're in for a surprise the next time you go on the trail."

Jeanie looked over suspiciously. "Why's that?"

"Because your favorite spot has been ruined. Better start looking for another place to sulk."

"What do you mean?"

"I mean someone cut down the climbing tree."

"What?" Laurel's parents shouted in unison. The loudness of their voices made Laurel start to feel uncomfortable about her announcement.

And Jeanie's face was awful to watch. Her expression changed slowly: first suspicion, then horror, and finally, complete misery. Then she disappeared from the room.

"Laurel! Is this true? Did you have to tell Jeanie in such a… well, why so mean, Laurel?" Her mother's voice was quieter now but still not normal, somehow tighter than normal.

"What do you mean, 'so mean'? I'm just telling you what I saw!" Silence.

Mrs. Shade finally ended it. "Laurel. You know that tree was really special to Jeanie. Why are you trying to make her feel bad?"

"The tree was special to me, too! You're acting like Jeanie owned it or something."

"Everybody loved that tree," her father said. "So what happened?"

"I don't know. Some new guy cut it down," Laurel answered. "Some guy named Holyfield."

"Holyfield," Dr. Shade repeated. Then there was another silence—a really long, awful silence.

Jeanie didn't reappear until bedtime. When she came into the bedroom, her eyes had a shutting-out look.

Laurel figured that Jeanie had gone to see the tree. She pictured little Jeanie standing there alone in the dusk, her brown hair all scraggly, her pointy little face all sad, her large eyes staring, fixed on that painful dark disk where the climbing tree had been.

The picture brought an ache to Laurel's throat. She suddenly wanted to comfort her sister. "How's it going?" she asked.

Jeanie didn't answer. The only sound was the drone of the window fan.

Laurel took a deep breath. She wondered about the best way to deal with Jeanie right now.

Jeanie wasn't the easiest sister—that was for sure. Their parents had even taken her to psychologists, not once but twice. The results were the same both times: Jeanie was not disturbed, they'd said. She was just an individual. Just highly creative. She knew the difference between real and pretend.

So why did she pretend she didn't? Was she trying to win some weirdness contest? It could be so infuriating. And yet whenever Laurel was ready to explode at her, Jeanie would suddenly seem breakable and alone. Then Laurel's heart would go out to her. Like now.

"Have you started packing for vacation yet?" Laurel asked hopefully.

Again, no answer. Just the droning fan.

The whole time they were getting ready for bed, Jeanie didn't talk. And as soon as they got into bed, Jeanie turned and faced the wall, even though the light was still on.

Laurel's gaze drifted around the room. The Shade house was fairly small by Chestnut Knoll standards, but the girls' bedroom was spacious—in an odd, long-and-narrow way. It had plenty of windows, too. Hard to complain too much about sharing a room when it happened to be the biggest, lightest one in the house. Laurel looked at the pale yellow walls and tried without success to call up a picture of how the room had looked before it was painted yellow.

Still not a word from Jeanie. Laurel felt bad. "Anything good on your television right now?" she asked, trying to sound casual.

Jeanie didn't respond for a long time. Finally, in a quiet, flat voice, she said, "No." But after a while she added, "Nothing good."

That was a little encouraging. Laurel decided to push further. "What *is* on?"

Another very long pause. "Just *The Skunky and Splat Show*."

Laurel felt an unexpected wave of happiness. "Oh really? What's that all about?"

"Well, tonight all they're doing is reading poems from their book," Jeanie said.

"They wrote a book? What's it called?"

"It's called *Skunky and Splat's Rotten Rhymes*."

"Could they read some to both of us?" Laurel asked. "Because you know I write poetry, too."

But Jeanie suddenly turned her back again. "No," she said.

"Why not?" Laurel tried to make her voice extra gentle, but she'd already pushed too far.

"Just no," Jeanie said to the wall. Laurel turned out the light and sank into her pillows.

A minute later Jeanie's voice floated through the darkness. "And besides. Those poems are *too gross*."

Tomorrow might be better, Laurel thought.

chapter 2

From a distance it looks like a tree from a fairy-tale forest. It actually has several trunks, and they twist out and around one another. The limbs could almost be human, the way they seem to squirm and wave and practically bend down to offer a foothold.

Standing right underneath, you can really see why it's called the climbing tree. The bark is corky, with cracks so deep you can dig your toes in easily. And in spite of their twists, the branches are so level to the ground and so evenly spaced they can be climbed like the rungs of a ladder.

Laurel pulls herself into the tree. It's effortless—she's practically floating from branch to branch. She reaches her favorite limb, the one that looks like a grazing animal. She straddles it and gently bounces, leaning forward. This is the way she imagines horseback riding. Totally free. But wait a second. Didn't someone cut the tree down? This must be a dream.

Laurel keeps climbing, though. She's heading for the top. But now people are rushing toward the tree. One of them is her father. "It's about to crash," he's shouting. "It's going to

Leave that computer alone! You crashed the whole system,
Laurel. All my data."

This *is* a dream, definitely, and now it's ending.

Laurel stared at the bumpy, sun-splotched ceiling, pulling herself
up from the dream. Then she flashed on the climbing tree and that
slightly sick feeling came back. Had it really happened? Had someone really cut it down? If only *that* were the dream.

She rolled over and looked out the window. The Chestnut
Knoll parents had begun their march to the train, which would
take them to their jobs in New York City. They did it at the same
time every morning. The Parent Parade, Laurel called it.

Everyone in the Parent Parade looked worried about something. And they were all in serious uniform: Suits. Buttoned-up
shirts. Briefcases. Most of the moms wore sneakers. But the sneakers didn't seem to belong on the feet of these grim-
looking women who marched past clipped lawns.

Jeanie was still sleeping when Laurel headed downstairs. She
stopped when she saw her mother.

Mrs. Shade described herself as a "happy former banker" or,
sometimes, as a "former unhappy banker." She had dropped out of
the Parent Parade about three years earlier and was now a stay-at-
home mom. She liked to say her new ambition was to be a gar-
dener, but that might be one of her little jokes.

Laurel's mother was elegant and tall—noticeably taller than her
husband, which some of Laurel's friends found remarkable. Laurel
thought of her mother as quick and funny and mostly nice, but not
gentle like Dr. Shade. "She's got a bit of an edge to her," Laurel had
once overheard another woman say about Mrs. Shade. Every so
often Laurel would think back to that remark. Her mother would
say something that made Laurel laugh, but had a little sting in it,

too. *Aha!* Laurel would say to herself. *There's that bit of an edge of hers.*

Her mother didn't look edgy now, though. She looked sad. She was sitting on a barstool at the kitchen island, staring into the distance. Her fingers drummed mournfully on the counter.

Laurel plopped herself onto a barstool. "Hi," she offered in a low, scratchy morning voice that surprised her.

Her mother answered, "Hi yourself" in a flat way. Then silence. Just drumming fingers.

Laurel stared down at the countertop. The previous night's bleakness started seeping back. She remembered the sound of her mother's voice saying, *"Why so mean, Laurel?"*

"I wanted to say—" Laurel started, then cleared the final scratches out of her voice. "I'm sorry about last night. I hope you're not mad or anything."

Her mother's hand scuttled over the countertop and covered Laurel's. "Honey, I'm not mad. We were all just kind of thrown off-balance."

"But you look upset or something."

"I was just thinking about…well, we're not going to Bar Harbor," Mrs. Shade said abruptly. "I need to cancel our reservations. Dad and I talked about it this morning. You know, his book put him way behind on all his other work. He says he's just too busy for Bar Harbor this year. In fact, he's at his office now. And with all the driving and everything, I don't think we could go on vacation without him. I mean, I can't even picture it."

"But I already started packing! We're supposed to leave tomorrow!"

"Laurel, I know. That was the plan. We're going to lose our hotel deposit, that's for sure."

Wow. Bombshell. The Shades went to Bar Harbor, Maine, for the last week of every summer. Except this one, apparently.

And wait a second, this vacation was supposed to be *extra-*

special. Laurel's birthday had come and gone a month ago, and they hadn't done anything about it. Laurel's mother had proposed that they wait until Dr. Shade's book was done—until Bar Harbor—to celebrate. And now she didn't even remember. Disappointment began rising in Laurel like a slow bubble.

From somewhere in the background came the word "kitten."

Kitten? Laurel's head jerked up. Her feet started swinging. "What did you say again?" she asked.

"Please don't kick the wood. I was asking how you would feel about getting a kitten."

A kitten. Cool!

"A kitten! Cool!" The words described Laurel's feelings, but they hadn't come from her. They came from behind her. From Jeanie.

Laurel and her mother swiveled around. Jeanie stood in the kitchen doorway, smiling. Jeanie hardly ever smiled, but when she did it was like a starburst. If someone had said, "Describe joy," Laurel would have answered, "Jeanie smiling."

"Hello, little J," her mother said. "Sleep okay?"

"Extremely okay, thank you," Jeanie said in an elaborately patient voice. "So *are we going to get a kitten*?"

Laurel's mother hesitated. "That's what Laurel and I were just talking about."

Jeanie literally bounced around the kitchen, the starburst smile now turned up full blast. "We're getting a kitten, we're getting a kitten!" she began chanting. "My dream came true!"

"Let's understand something." Mrs. Shade cleared her throat. "This kitten... listen, we still have to check with Dad. But if we get a kitten, it will really be Laurel's. She's old enough to take care of it. Besides, we never really celebrated her birthday this year. We were going to do something for her birthday in Bar Harbor, but now it turns out we can't go."

Everything about Jeanie slowed: the bounce, the smile, the chanting. *It's like her TV just got paused,* Laurel thought. She felt her own happiness dip.

"It can be partly your kitten, too," Laurel said to Jeanie. Then, as the starburst returned to its full splendor, Laurel proclaimed, "It will be *all* of ours."

"Well, in that case," Mrs. Shade said, "I guess I'd better give Dad the news."

When their mother came back from the phone, the girls pushed up to her, both talking loudly at the same time. Mrs. Shade closed her eyes as if in pain.

"Please stop pushing and be quiet," she said. "Well, guess what. Your father doesn't want a kitten. He said he's always secretly hated cats."

That night the Shades had dinner at Lilacs, their favorite restaurant. It was Mrs. Shade's idea. Her thought was that going out to eat might soothe some feelings. But they'd waited more than half an hour to be seated. And when they finally got a table, it seemed too squeezed, and too noisy to talk, except in loud, tense declarations.

"I thought restaurants were supposed to be so empty in August," Mrs. Shade said. "It's strange."

"Sure *is* strange," Laurel said bitterly. "Everyone else in Chestnut Knoll *goes on vacation* this time of year."

Abruptly, Jeanie spoke. "It *sucks* that we can't get a kitten. And it *sucks* that we're not going to Bar Harbor."

Her mother flashed back, like a reflex: "You know we don't say 'sucks' in this family."

"Okay, fine." Jeanie then began rhythmically pounding her silverware and chanting, "Bar HAR-bor, Bar HAR-bor…" Her mother just twitched her mouth back and forth.

Laurel pushed back in her chair, willing herself as far from the Shade table as possible. Just then someone's fingers danced on the table near Laurel's hand. "Howdy, pardner!"

It was Shannon McDermott, Laurel's good friend. She and her family were on their way out of the restaurant.

"Shannon! I thought you were on Martha's Vineyard!"

"We should be. We got back like three seconds ago. One of my mom's clients is involved in some kind of corporate invasion, so we had to come back really suddenly. Which really sucks, you know?" Shannon widened her eyes. "Oh, Laurel, I can't wait to tell you about the Vineyard!"

Shannon's almost-elbow-length hair looked even lighter and silkier than usual. Her face was golden pink and dusted with freckles. She gestured in her parents' direction and made a comically stifled expression, gagging herself with one hand. "Call me tomorrow!" she whispered to Laurel.

The girls' mothers had been chatting politely. Now Mrs. McDermott's voice suddenly turned agitated. "Say, Beth, don't you live right near the old cork tree that some lunatic just cut down?"

Silence. Then memories were swimming through Laurel's head. She was suddenly remembering how she and Shannon and Jackie Fiedler used to leave messages for each other tucked into the bark of the climbing tree. That was back in second grade, before Jackie moved away, of course. Now the tree was gone, too.

"Imagine cutting down something that had lived so long," Laurel's mother was saying.

"Especially a tree that wasn't even on your own property! A tree in a nature preserve!" Shannon's mom was indignant. "Of course, it wasn't anyone from Chestnut Knoll or anything. I heard it was some guy from someplace else, from Pennsylvania or someplace."

"Oh really," said Mrs. Shade.

"Yes," Shannon's mother said. "I don't know the name."

"*Holyfield.*" Jeanie had spoken up in an odd shrill voice. "The name is Holyfield."

The rest of the Shades were silent and looked down at the tablecloth, as if someone had said *manslaughter* or *cancer.* The McDermotts, looking grim, filed out of the restaurant.

Now Laurel found herself remembering a summer night when Shannon had come for a sleepover, and the two of them had sneaked out very late to the climbing tree. She remembered their flashlights slicing the dark, the thrill of pulling up into the tree, the feel of the wind with its summer smells. And the lightning bugs were amazing, flashing all around them and then rising, almost blending with the twinkling stars.

All at once Laurel was yearning for that night. If only it could come back. If only Laurel could go to the trail on a different day or walk a slightly different path and the tree would be there. It was finally sinking in, for some reason, only this very moment: the climbing tree wasn't just gone. It would never be there again. A thick feeling came into her throat.

Then a poetic inspiration was upon her. She made a quick, urgent hunt for a pen. The poem seemed to write itself on her grease-splotched paper napkin.

> *I think I'll never feel as free*
> *As I used to in the climbing tree.*
> *That tree took me to Zanzibar*
> *And other places strange and far*
> *And to a special star way up in the sky—*
> *Once the tree was gone, I saw how high.*

The car ride home from the restaurant was quiet. From the front seat, Mrs. Shade sighed. "It seems like it's getting dark too early," she said.

Then Laurel heard her mother breathe in sharply. "There it is," Mrs. Shade said. "Norman, did you come this way on purpose?"

"What way? We're just going home," Dr. Shade said, but there they were, stopped at the point where the nature trail came closest to the street, the point where the climbing tree used to be visible from the road.

"I never noticed that little white house before," Mrs. Shade said.

"Of course not," said Dr. Shade quietly. "You couldn't see it when the tree was there."

"Daddy, are you trying to make us feel worse? It's like everything's being taken away!" Laurel had intended a dignified statement of grievance, but her voice had gone all quavering and whiny. "First the tree, and then Bar Harbor, and then…"

"Will you please be quiet?" Jeanie shouted. "Be quiet, be *quiet,* I am *trying* to watch the *Kitten Channel!*"

Dr. Shade turned around and glared. When he exhaled, he made a small exploding sound. "You girls are wearing me down," he said. Then he turned back around and started the car again.

When their father got home the next day, he was carrying a large beige plastic box. After shouldering his way through the front door, he placed the box on the floor. Then he opened a metal gate on one end and reached inside. He lifted something out and held it cupped in his hands like a butterfly.

But it wasn't a butterfly. It was a kitten. A silky gray kitten. It stretched its neck up and peered out between Dr. Shade's thumbs. Its eyes were a startling silver.

Everyone was squealing at once. Jeanie's squeal rose above the others. "She's *adorable!* Let's call her Twinkle! Like Skunky and Splat's cat!"

"He's a boy," said Dr. Shade. "He's a boy, and his name is Nightshade."

chapter 3

Laurel decides to write a poem in honor of Nightshade's arrival.

> *Nightshade, beloved Nightshade,*

she says to herself,

> *Your love is sweeter than lemonade.*
> *Girls would wrestle tigers,*
> *Or walk on hot coals all night long,*
> *For just one little lick*
> *From your tiny sandpaper tongue.*

Never, Laurel thinks, has she been so inspired. She and Nightshade are going to have a mystical bond. She can already feel it. Nightshade will be her Old Yeller, her Friend Flicka.

Her heart is full. And it aches for every kid in the world who doesn't have a kitten.

But having Nightshade in their home brought its worries. As soon as Dr. Shade put him down, he dashed under the sofa and stayed huddled there, out of reach.

Laurel was distressed. "He doesn't seem very happy."

"Give him some time," said her mother. "Look, he's only seven weeks old. He's never been away from his mom before. It's a big adjustment."

Laurel thought about the first night she'd spent away from home. At bedtime she'd been overcome with an achy yearning, especially in her stomach. Homesick, she had realized. Sick for her own home. Poor little Nightshade—seven weeks old and all alone. Was it wrong to have taken him from his mother?

Just then Nightshade let out a frightened yowl. Jeanie had managed to grab his rear legs and was dragging him toward her.

"Jeanie, let go!" cried Mrs. Shade. "You're scaring him!"

"He loves me," Jeanie insisted, tightening her grip.

Laurel's anxiety made her voice shrill. "Let him go!"

Nightshade catapulted himself out of Jeanie's arms and under the sofa once more. Jeanie began to dive after him, but her mother grabbed her by the shoulders. "Everybody stop shouting! And everybody just leave Nightshade alone for a while!" Mrs. Shade was shouting herself.

Nightshade stayed under the sofa, out of arm's reach. Eventually things settled down. Laurel even briefly forgot that they had a kitten. As dinnertime approached, she began setting the table as if it were an ordinary evening instead of an evening when they had a kitten.

"You're supposed to help set the table," she reminded Jeanie.

"No no no, not now," Jeanie moaned. She was scrunched up on the sofa with her eyes closed. "I'm right in the middle of the Super Ball."

"Super Ball? Super *Ball*? What's that supposed to be?"

Jeanie snorted. "It's only the biggest football game of the year."

"You mean the Super *Bowl,* you cuckoohead."

"Super Bowl?" Jeanie repeated in disbelief. "You mean like a bowl of cereal?"

"Exactly," their mother called from the kitchen. "Except it's very large. And it's filled with grunting, sweating men instead of cereal."

A pause. Then Jeanie waved her hand impatiently. "Whatever. Anyway, the score is tied."

Laurel sighed and began counting knives and forks. For a fleeting moment she considered slipping off to the climbing tree—and then in the same moment remembered it was gone.

She and Jeanie had often made a quick trip to the tree before dinner. Sometimes you'd see five or six kids in it at once, hanging like ripe fruit; that's how perfect it was for climbing. Laurel would rush forward to join the crowd, laughing and scrambling for a space. But Jeanie's eyes would get the shutting-out look and she'd turn away. Somehow having other kids around spoiled the tree for Jeanie. And of course there was no other tree like it.

But why not?

"Mom, why aren't there any other cork trees around here? Why was the climbing tree the only one?"

Her mother looked at Laurel, puzzled. "Good question. Now you've got me curious."

Laurel reached into the lazy-Susan cabinet for the salt and pepper. As it clicked open and the shelves began their silent spinning, Nightshade streaked inside.

"Oh my God," Laurel gasped.

Her mother instantly said, "You know we don't say 'oh my God' in this family."

"But Nightshade's inside! He'll be crushed!"

Her mother grabbed the sides of the lazy Susan and stopped it. "He's all right," she said. "Calm down."

Jeanie raced over to the lazy Susan and flopped down on her stomach. "Come here, sweetie pie, I've got you," she called. "Don't worry, sweetie, I've got you now." Her voice was much higher and sillier-sounding than usual.

"Leave him alone," Laurel cried. "He's *my* cat."

"No," Jeanie said stubbornly. "You said he'd be all of ours. And I'm not going to let him die back there. C'mere, little sweetie pie," she called in her new high voice.

Nightshade did nothing. He couldn't even be seen, really. They could only be sure he was still there by the flashing of a silver eye every so often from the back of the cabinet.

"Come on, let's get on with supper," Laurel's mother finally said. "He's not going to die back there. He'll come out when he's ready."

Only much later, well after dessert, was Nightshade spotted. He was stepping delicately along the back of the sofa.

"There's Nightshade!" everyone cried at once. Jeanie made a grab for him, but he ducked under the sofa. Laurel ran to shut the door of the nightmare lazy Susan. As the door closed with its tiny, precise click, she felt as if she'd just put out a fire.

Later, as she lay in bed, Laurel thought a little sadly about the way she'd imagined her first night with a kitten. She had pictured a sweet, purring ball of fur nestling in her arms and staying there all night long. But instead, Nightshade had exiled himself to dusty loneliness under the sofa. Such *total* loneliness, too. No family. No playmates. Shunning those who longed to comfort him.

Well, tomorrow would be better. Laurel would stay near, ready to offer help but never selfishly snatching him up. And soon Nightshade would seek her out. He would rub his head against her hand and purr sweetly. He would truly be her kitten.

These tender thoughts were shattered by Jeanie's whisper. "Laurel, something is bothering me. Laurel? Why would someone want to cut down a tree in a nature preserve?"

"How am I supposed to know?"

"But there must be some kind of reason, right?"

"Jeanie, I have no idea. Unless—I don't know. Maybe if they lived right near that spot, and they wanted more space or more light or something for their own yard."

"That's all I can think of, too. That would be really selfish, wouldn't it?"

Laurel sighed. "Yes. Totally selfish."

"But if that's the only reason anyone would ever do it, that means that Holyfield guy must live right near us. Right near the tree. He must be our neighbor."

"Maybe," Laurel said. *Which one could be the Holyfield house?* she wondered just before sleep swallowed her.

chapter 4

O n her way to the kitchen the next morning, Laurel pauses at the door to the study. Something draws her to a paper lying on the computer keyboard.

The paper is heavily marked up—lots of underlining, lots of notes in the margins. It looks like the kind of thing her mother might print out from one of her online gardening classes. But then Laurel notices the heading at the top of the page: AMUR CORK TREE.

Underneath is a black-and-white photograph of a tree. The photo isn't very clear. But the tree is unmistakably the same kind as the climbing tree. The only difference is that its branches don't seem as twisty.

A particularly picturesque variety, the text says. *Normally reaches 40 feet at maturity, except for its dwarf species (considered rare). Branches are stout and strongly horizontal. Bark is thick and corky, developing deep fissures as the tree ages. Shiny, dark green oblong leaves, 10 to 15 inches long; very light, almost white, wood.*

The phrase about the "almost white" wood has been circled. Next to it is a handwritten note: ***Why is the stump so dark?***

Another portion of the text has been heavily underlined: *Native to northern China,* says the article. The margin says: **What's it doing in a New York nature preserve?**

It was weird, all right, Laurel thought. Nature preserves were supposed to be places where things just grew wild. Nobody cut things down, nobody planted there. How did a tree from northern China make its way there by itself? Laurel decided to look for her mom and ask her about it.

Then a squeaking sound caught her ear. Laurel turned. Nightshade, tiny, silky, was stretching at the bottom of the stairs, his silver eyes reflecting the sun. The sight of him took her breath away.

She squatted down, delighted. A nonhuman sound, part trill, part purr, magically started up in her chest.

Nightshade started creeping toward her. Then he hesitated. He hung back just out of reach.

Laurel kept up the magical trilling. She began stroking the rug with the tips of her fingers. As if under a spell, Nightshade moved forward once more.

Laurel reached toward him, slowly, delicately. Love surged into her throat. This would be the first time that Nightshade had let anyone touch him.

Then Jeanie was bouncing down the stairs. "I want to hold him!" She rushed toward Nightshade, hands grasping.

Nightshade disappeared under a chair.

A wave of rage crashed over Laurel. "You just spoiled everything!" She jerked her head around and glared at Jeanie.

To her surprise, Jeanie's face was a picture of misery. Jeanie cried even more rarely than she smiled. But this look, right now, was very close to crying.

Now their mother swept into the room. "How's everyone doing this morning?" She squinted at their faces. "What's wrong?

You girls aren't torturing that poor kitten, are you?"

The only response was a painful silence.

"Well?" their mother said after a moment.

"Nothing," Jeanie said abruptly. "Come on outside, Laurel. I want to show you something."

Laurel hesitated. She wanted to say she didn't feel like it. But her mother gave her an edgy look and cut her off. "Go on, Laurel. I need to get some work done in here."

Jeanie led Laurel down near the spot where the climbing tree had been.

"That's got to be the house," Jeanie said in a low voice. "The Holyfield house."

She pointed to a small white-shingled house, almost shabby-looking. It was the house Laurel had noticed on the day she had first seen the tree stump. With the tree gone, the house had been opened up to light and space.

Both girls gazed at the house in silence. Then Jeanie's warm breath was filling Laurel's ear. "I'm going to look for that Holyfield guy," she whispered, and was gone.

Fear rose. *Come back here right now!* Laurel's brain screamed. But she didn't dare make a sound. Then she saw Jeanie's head below a window, peering into the little house.

Trespass, that's what this was. *Trespass*—people didn't even say the word in their normal voices. They were trespassing against the property of the man who cut down the climbing tree.

What sort of man must he be? He wasn't hesitant, that was for sure. He had just swept in and destroyed the climbing tree.

Laurel tried to imagine his face. For some reason she pictured a bald head with cold fish eyes blinking slowly. An electric tingle spiraled down her body. Her legs became oddly motorized, turning her around and carrying her rapidly to her own yard.

Then she heard Jeanie's whisper behind her. *"Wait for me, Laurel, wait up."*

Laurel paused, expectant. But when Jeanie came up next to her, all she did was smile mysteriously.

"Well, did you see the man?" Laurel prodded.

"No."

"Why are you smiling like that? Did you see anything?"

"Yes." Once more, the mysterious smile. Nothing more.

"Jean-NEEY! What did you see?"

"I saw a girl."

"A girl?"

"Yeah. She had this really long dark ponytail and glasses. And she was looking for something." A long pause. "She was looking for something inside her computer."

Laurel was exasperated. "Jeanie, what are you talking about?"

"I told you. She was *looking* for something. She looked upset. She was using a computer. And she would type something, and then she'd stare at the screen like she was looking for something really hard but not finding it. Then she'd type some more and stare some more and look even more upset. So I think something's lost inside that computer. I wonder what it is."

And then they were walking through their own back door.

Laurel and Shannon McDermott had just finished lunch. Laurel had told Shannon over the phone that they'd gotten the world's most wonderful kitten, and Shannon had squealed, and said how jealous she was, and begged to come over for lunch so she could see.

But now Nightshade was plainly not meeting Shannon's expectations. He had once more turned himself into an immobile gray ball under the sofa.

"I thought you said he was so great," Shannon said after a few minutes.

"He is," Laurel said quickly. "He just hasn't gotten used to you."

"Well, what about *you*? He's not being any friendlier to you."

Laurel wanted to protest, but Shannon definitely had a point. Nightshade gave no sign of friendliness. He had stayed at his lonely outpost under the sofa ever since Jeanie's morning grab.

Maybe he was homesick. Maybe he missed his mom. An image of Nightshade curled up blissfully next to a larger version of himself flashed through Laurel's head. She felt a guilty pang.

Then she pushed the image aside and groped for something else to focus on. His food. "Maybe his food could be the problem," she said.

"Absolutely!" Shannon's agreement was surprisingly forceful. "I think you need to buy him a different kind."

It was that emptied-out part of summer when most of the families were away somewhere. A person could walk for blocks without seeing a soul. Every so often an in-line skater would whiz past. Otherwise the day was still, and so hot that the air above the pavement looked wavy.

Laurel wore a backpack for bringing the cat food home. The skin under her backpack dripped. "These backpacks really make your back sweat, don't they?" she complained.

Shannon stared at Laurel with distaste. Then she crinkled her lightly freckled nose and groaned. "Ga-*ross*!" She tossed her blond hair. Something like shame flushed through Laurel.

The first store they reached was a small convenience mart. "Let's not go in that place—I hate that place," Shannon urged. Laurel hated it, too. The store was run by a husband and wife who were always arguing. And Laurel always seemed to get mysteriously drawn into their quarrels. She couldn't ask where the marshmallows were without the husband snarling at his wife, "I told you we needed more marshmallows!"

They also bypassed the big drugstore. Shannon and another friend had recently worn in-line skates inside and had been asked to leave in a very rude way, according to Shannon.

Eventually they reached Cleve's Corner Store. Cleve's was a small store, but huge in the lives of Chestnut Knoll's middle graders.

Cleve, the owner, had uninviting looks: broad red face, bald head, squinty eyes. But inside was the soul of Santa Claus. He knew most of the kids by name—"Lovely Laurel of the Shade variety" was what he always called Laurel. And he loaded up his store with comic books and candy.

But the store's appeal went deeper. A halo of coolness surrounded Cleve's. It didn't have much in the way of cat food. But it was totally cool.

"Well, hello, ladies," someone said in a Donald Duck voice.

It was Collin and Marcus, two boys from Tuckerman, and they were grinning and pacing like untrained puppies.

Laurel looked over at Shannon. Shannon was showily tossing her hair and crinkling her nose. Then came the realization, like a thunderbolt: Cleve's had been Shannon's destination all along.

"So what's up?" Collin had dropped the Donald Duck routine, but he was still grinning and pacing. "School's starting in like a week or something, huh? Bet you can't wait."

"Yeah right, Collin," Shannon said. "If you say so."

"Did you guys hear about the climbing tree getting the ax?" Collin bugged his eyes out. "Some guy from Pittsburgh or something. My dad was really steamed. He was like, 'The guy who did that ought to be run out of town.' Pretty amazing, huh?"

The conversation now had a strange, familiar feeling—had Laurel dreamed it once? *Pretty amazing, huh; pretty amazing, huh.* Laurel repeated the words to herself until she saw a picture of the freckled boy with the huge gray teeth. *This is just like when I heard about the climbing tree,* she realized. The memory was remarkably powerful. She could almost smell the trail.

Meanwhile, the conversation had shifted. The boys were saying something about Japan.

Laurel felt confused. "Wait. Why are you talking about Japan?" she asked.

"*Duh,* Laurel," Shannon said. She flashed a pained look at the boys. "They *just said* Yuriko went back to Japan."

Oh no. No, not Yuriko!

Yuriko had come to school the year before, brand-new to America. She couldn't speak English. Her hair was so black it glistened rainbows.

Yuriko had sat at her desk with her head down, looking so shy that Laurel ached just watching. During her first recess, Yuriko had sat alone on the playground on the far stone wall, where no one ever hung out.

Laurel had approached as carefully as if Yuriko were a baby deer. But then she hadn't known what to say. So that night, after thinking for quite a while, she'd written a little poem.

> *We don't talk the same,*
> *We look different too,*
> *But somehow I think*
> *I will still like you.*

She had put it on Yuriko's chair the next morning. Face down so no one else could see.

The next day a drawing had been waiting for her. It was astonishing; it was real art. She could even recognize the face—it was her own. There was the shoulder-length light brown hair, the almond-shaped blue-green eyes, the pointed chin, the long limbs. But it was a Laurel that might be in movies. Her eyes looked like aquamarine gemstones surrounded by thick lashes. Her hair was swirling and sprinkled with gold. Her body suggested confidence and grace.

Laurel had looked at Yuriko in wonder. Yuriko had given her a melting smile.

That was the beginning of their secret friendship. All that year they'd exchanged private smiles, poems, and small gifts. Yuriko's drawings were so remarkable that Laurel kept them in a special box. No one knew about their friendship. That was part of its magic.

Now this magic friend was gone! "Why?" Laurel asked woefully, out loud.

Her three companions in Cleve's looked puzzled.

"Why did she go back to Japan?" Laurel said.

"Laurel! Puh-leeze!" Shannon sounded totally disgusted. "You are like *such* a space cadet!"

"You still talking about Yuriko?" Marcus said. "They left 'cause she and her family hated it here, that's why. None of them made any friends."

"No friends?" Laurel repeated uneasily.

"That's what I said. No friends. Zero. Zilch."

"It wouldn't have hurt to speak English," Shannon said sarcastically. The boys laughed.

I do not want to be here. Laurel realized it all at once. Something strange and slightly unpleasant was going on. The boys were acting strange—why did they keep just hanging around like this? Shannon was acting strange, too—not much like a best friend. She was acting like she didn't even like Laurel. *So why on God's green earth am I staying here,* Laurel abruptly asked herself, *being made to feel like a fool?*

"I better get going," she said out loud. Shannon looked over at Marcus and Collin and rolled her eyes.

And Cleve was looking expectantly at Laurel. He had just asked her for fourteen-something for the cat food, and all she'd brought was a ten-dollar bill.

"You don't have the money?" Shannon's voice was horrified, and pitched loud enough that the boys were sure to hear. "Laurel! That is so *not cool!*"

But Cleve cut Shannon off. "No problem, Lovely Laurel," he said. "Just ask your folks to stop by and drop off the rest. Besides, I have something I'd like them to sign." He pointed to a clipboard on the countertop.

We hereby demand that the Town Conservation Board investigate the destruction of a historic tree located on town property, began the paper on the clipboard. It went on for two or three paragraphs and then had spaces for signatures. It was already nearly full.

"See you later, ladies," Collin called on his way out.

"Not if I see you first," Shannon shouted. Then she turned to Laurel. "C'mon, let's go to my parents' club. I'll call my house-keeper. She can come get us and drive us there."

"I've got to go," Laurel said quietly.

"Did I tell you the club has a trampoline now?" Shannon gave Laurel's arm a cajoling tug. Laurel ignored it.

Shannon smiled the smile that made her dimples show. "Come on, Laurel! *Please* come with me! It'll be *so,* so cool."

An hour earlier the offer would have been welcome. But now Laurel was smarting too much to feel tempted. She had been to Shannon's parents' club before—she had even been on the tram-poline. It wasn't really *so,* so cool, Laurel told herself. And why was Shannon acting so much nicer now that no one else was around?

No friends. Zero. Zilch. The words kept bobbing up in Laurel's brain as she headed home. She'd told herself that she was Yuriko's secret friend—but *why had she wanted it secret?* And how could it be that

Yuriko had had no other friends and Laurel had *never even noticed*? A knot was tying itself inside her stomach.

At the same time a memory kept trying to push into her head, and she kept trying to push it back without actually looking at it. Finally it just shoved inside and Laurel had to stare it in the face.

It was a memory of a conversation with Shannon after Laurel had first met Yuriko. Laurel was talking about Yuriko. Shannon had acted more and more restless. Then she had cut in. "I mean, it's not like you'd be really good friends with a Japanese girl," Shannon had said.

Why not? had been Laurel's first confused reaction. But she had just nodded in a vague kind of way—a vague kind of way that practically said "Of course not." Now Yuriko was gone. *No friends. Zero. Zilch.*

This was really not a good feeling. Too late now, of course.

If only Laurel could go back and do things differently. If only she could have a second chance. She was definitely going to be a better person from now on. She'd be compassionate. Fearless. She'd be the kind of kid who... who'd stand up to Nazis—yes, Nazis.

But Yuriko was still gone.

Laurel really just wanted to be home. By herself. Holding Nightshade.

Laurel pushed her way through her front door, full of resolve.

She gasped.

Nightshade was curled up in Jeanie's arms. He was purring.

Jeanie gave Laurel a broad, self-satisfied smile.

Laurel's face felt tight and hot. There seemed to be a faint hum in her ears. *I will not stay here,* she thought. *I refuse to live for one more day in the same house as Jeanie.*

Laurel bolted out of the house and ran down the trail. She ran without feeling her legs. Then a tree root grabbed her foot and sent her sprawling.

Laurel pulled herself onto a boulder at the side of the trail. She stared at her stinging hands for a long time. *Am I going to throw up?* she wondered. *Am I having a dream right now?*

She wondered where she could go instead of home.

She thought about this bitter ending to the story of her kitten. The kitten she had wanted all these years. It was so blindingly unjust. That *Jeanie* should have won the heart of the new kitten.

Something touched her leg. She shuddered and looked up into her father's face. He was sitting next to her. His eyes looked worried.

"What are you doing here?" The words flew out of Laurel's mouth just as she was thinking she would never speak to anyone in her family ever again.

"Apparently while I was popping in the front door, you were popping out the back," her father answered. His voice was teasing, but his eyes still looked worried. "Your mom thought you'd be on the trail somewhere. And *voilà,* here you are."

"Oh, Daddy," Laurel said. It came out sounding babyish. She closed her eyes.

"Tell me everything that happened," her father suggested.

And out it came. How she'd longed for a kitten for so many years. How she'd looked forward to Nightshade sleeping in her bed, and then Jeanie had spoiled all that. How Jeanie had also spoiled the morning with Nightshade. How Laurel had made a special trip to get food for Nightshade, and heard about Yuriko, and vowed to be a better person, and hurried home to comfort Nightshade....

"And while I was gone, Jeanie was busy stealing my kitten away from me! It is so totally unfair!"

Dr. Shade just looked thoughtful.

"I've been following all the rules," Laurel continued. "Nightshade was so scared yesterday when he first got home and Mom said to leave him alone, so I did. I followed the rules. But

Jeanie just ignored all that and kept snatching him and calling him 'sweetie pie' like he was hers...."

Laurel's voice was getting louder. She was practically shouting. "She's probably been sneaking him chocolates!" she said wildly. "Just so he'll love her more than me. She never follows the rules, and neither of you *ever... Nobody ever does anything about it!*"

"Okay, Laurel, okay," her father was saying. He grabbed her waving hands. "I love it that you're so passionate and everything. But sometimes you really blow things out of proportion. Now I want you to hear me out. Mom said that when you guys were talking about getting a kitten, you told Jeanie it could be partly hers. You wanted to be generous. You *are* generous. But if you put yourself in Jeanie's shoes for a minute, well, isn't she really just acting like the kitten *is* partly hers? That doesn't seem so outrageous."

"*Partly* hers—not *mostly* hers! She knows Nightshade was really meant for me!"

"Hear me out, Laurel. Look, here's my understanding of your day. One friend came for lunch, and you went to the store together. When you got there, you met up with two more friends, who gave you the latest news about yet another friend..."

"Marcus and Collin aren't friends—they're just boys in my class," Laurel said hotly. "And Yuriko's back in Japan, so she doesn't count. And Shannon, well..." Laurel trailed off, troubled, remembering Shannon's odd hostility.

"Laurel, please. You get my point. Now think for a minute about who Jeanie's friends are."

At that particular moment Laurel couldn't think of any. "She's only seven," she finally said.

"As I recall, you had quite a few friends even at age seven."

"Well, then... you know, Jeanie doesn't even want friends, she's got her television!"

Dr. Shade's mouth twisted. "You talk about wanting to be a

better person, Laurel, but charity begins at home, right? Why don't you notice that Jeanie really could use a friend?"

Heat rushed to Laurel's face. She stared fiercely at the ground. Of course. Of course! As usual, for the trillionth time, her parents were catering to Jeanie. Laurel's whole world might be cracking—she could be aching, dying—and her parents would still cater to Jeanie.

Dr. Shade tilted Laurel's chin up, trying vainly to make eye contact. "I'm not saying you're not a good kid, Laurel—you know you are. You're incredibly kind and decent and sensitive. All I'm trying to say is that Jeanie is one of the most *alone* people I can think of, and you... well, you're one of the most liked. Look, Laurel, I know a kitten's love means a lot to you. But just think how precious it must be to Jeanie."

"So what do you expect me to do?"

"Will you try to be generous with your sister about this kitten business?"

For a tiny moment her father's voice seemed to shake. It was weird to see him this serious. How could she disagree with him now?

"Okay, Dad," she mumbled. But her heart was not at peace.

"Thanks, Laurel." Then, after an awkward pause: "Would you like to walk back with me now?"

Laurel hesitated. "Well..."

Her father started to chuckle. He was sounding like his usual self again. "Okay," he said, and tousled her hair. "I'm not looking for a miracle. Just please try." He stood up, brushed off his pants, and walked ahead of her up the trail.

That night Nightshade padded into the girls' bedroom. He climbed up on Jeanie's bed.

Laurel's heart knotted. She watched Nightshade make three or four small circles and then nestle down just behind Jeanie's knees.

Laurel turned to lie facing the wall.

I don't care, she tried to tell herself, but she knew it wasn't true.

I wish we'd never gotten a kitten, she thought as a hot tear rolled into her nostril.

chapter 5

Just one week later and Laurel is standing at the back of a classroom, holding a stack of notebooks against her chest. *It can't really be the first day of school,* she is thinking. Summer had somehow convinced her that it would never end. Now, in a single morning, it is dissolving like cotton candy in her mouth.

Sixth grade! The classroom looks huge. The students are in a tangle at the back, waiting for their seat assignments. A few new faces stand out. Mostly it's the same familiar Tuckerman School kids, though.

But today even the old-timers look a little different. Strange haircuts. Teenagery clothes. Some kids seem several years older than they did in June. Even Sarah Teller and Chrissie Paradiso, whom Laurel has seen over the summer, have a different sheen today.

Now Mrs. Gombiner is calling out names, one by one, and pointing to each student's assigned seat.

"Applebaum."

"Barr."

"Davies."

With each name that is called, the tangle at the back of the room titters a little and then disgorges a student.

"Enders."

"Endo."

Those two names, Enders and Endo, have followed each other on student lists for as long as Laurel can remember. Had they ever been pried apart? Could anyone ever squeeze between them?

"Forest."

"Greene."

"Greenfeld."

This class roll is kind of funny if you pay attention. Why, it's practically a word game.

"Holyfield."

No titter this time, just silence.

A tall boy with floppy light brown hair and a long arched nose appears from the back of the tangle. His face looks lean, angular. He holds a backpack by its straps with one wrist, and the wrist looks lean and angular, too.

Most of the students are staring openly. Something in Laurel's head has started whirring.

The silence continues. Finally Mrs. Gombiner clears her throat. "David Holyfield. First year at Tuckerman?" she says.

Laurel can't see the boy anymore—too many heads in the way. She doesn't hear an answer. But he must have nodded, because Mrs. Gombiner continues the roll.

"Immer."

"Latimer."

"Madison."

Laurel can't keep her mind on the roll anymore. She stretches and twists to see the boy.

Mrs. Gombiner finally calls, "Shade." Laurel's heart starts beating faster. She feels a sudden fearful hunch. What if she is made to sit near that Holyfield boy?

Mrs. Gombiner points to Laurel's desk. It is close to the boy, kitty-corner from him.

A violent shudder travels down Laurel's back. She turns and looks at Sarah Teller in panic.

"Could be worse," Sarah mouths. Laurel sits down.

It would be a very short week—just Thursday and Friday—and this first-day class was also very short. Almost as soon as the students took their seats, it seemed, it was time to leave. They poured out into the hall, laughing and talking loudly. Someone did a cartwheel, right in the thick of things. Felicity Osterman, of course. Felicity was addicted to cartwheels.

The only quiet zone was the space surrounding the new boy, the Holyfield boy. He was like a magnet pointed the wrong way, pushing all the other magnets back.

Laurel hung back from him, too. But she couldn't stop watching. He was standing in front of one of the cubbies. He took out a sheet of turquoise paper. Could someone have left him a note? He read it without his face changing at all. Then he stuck it in his notebook.

He looked up and then toward the exit, and it was the first time Laurel had seen his face up close. There was something strange about his eyes. They were strangely light, greenish gray, almost greenish white. They didn't look like normal human eyes. They were as unreadable as a cat's.

Suddenly his head swiveled and he was looking right at Laurel. Laurel pivoted away and intently studied the cubby next to her. A lopsided ghost rose up at the back of the cubby, where someone had traced the wood grain with a felt-tip pen.

Then he was heading down the hallway, his backpack held at one side by an angular wrist.

As Laurel walked to her own cubby, she saw several other students holding sheets of turquoise paper. There was one in Laurel's cubby, too. There was one in every cubby in the school.

Laurel pulled it out and read it. **ONLY GOD CAN MAKE A TREE,** it said.

The Westchester Ever Green Group (WEGG)
invites all parents to its first
meeting of the fall

When: Sept. 22 at 7:30 P.M.
Where: Chestnut Knoll Library
meeting room
Subject: Protecting our precious Westchester
wilderness areas:
Are stronger laws or stricter
enforcement needed to protect the
Chestnut Knoll Nature Trail?

★ **PLEASE COME** ★
★ **SHARPEN YOUR AWARENESS** ★
★ **WELCOME BACK** ★
WEGG: The Organization for Westchester
Families and the Environment

After she finished reading the turquoise paper, Laurel stretched for a final glimpse of the Holyfield boy, but he was gone.

Laurel and Shannon were assigned to different classes, but last night Shannon had called and suggested they walk home together. Laurel was wary at first, remembering the scornful, cutting Shannon of Cleve's. But the telephone Shannon of last night was so warm and casual that it seemed impossible anything had soured. And now, as they met at the main doorway, Shannon was brimming with silliness and sunny goodwill. She kept calling Laurel "pardner."

They stopped off at Jeanie's second-grade classroom, because Laurel had promised to walk her sister home. All the second graders seemed to be chattering or greeting parents. Except Jeanie. She was in a corner of the room with the teacher. The teacher looked serious.

But then Jeanie looked up and waved. She skipped over to Laurel and Shannon. "Home, James," she said breezily.

On the way home, Laurel and Shannon hung back so that no one could tell they were walking with a second grader. Jeanie walked a house and a half ahead. For some reason, she looked very thin as she walked alone in front of them. Maybe it was because she was wearing a dress for a change.

"You won't believe who's in my class—a new kid named Holyfield," Laurel said. "That's the family that chopped down the climbing tree!"

"No she isn't—she's in mine!" Shannon cried out.

"Wait a second. It's not a girl, it's a boy." Laurel was baffled.

"Listen, Laurel, there's a new girl in my class named Holyfield! I mean, it's not like I'd make this up or something."

"Well, there's a boy named Holyfield in mine. How can there be two new kids in sixth grade named Holyfield? It must be the same family," Laurel decided. "They must be twins."

"No—I've got it!" Shannon crossed her eyes and stuck her tongue out of a corner of her mouth. "One of them flunked! That's why they're in the same grade!" She let out a loud, juicy pig snort.

Then Shannon grabbed Laurel's arm, laughing hard, and practically fell against her. She made the pig-snorting sound again, this time even louder and juicier.

Laurel was laughing, too. She stopped and gasped and held her sides—that's how hard she was laughing.

As soon as Dr. Shade's car pulled in that night, Laurel and Jeanie rushed out to the driveway.

"Well, how nice of you to meet me out here," their father said.

"Yes, yes, pleasure to meet you," Jeanie responded, pumping his hand up and down. "How do you do, how do you do."

"We had school today, Dad," Laurel said, trying to sound particularly grown-up. "Something kind of exciting happened."

"My teacher wants me to skip a grade! She thinks I should be in third grade!" Jeanie shouted.

Laurel stared at her sister. Where did she come up with these things? "Shut up, you little fibber!" she said indignantly.

Immediately, she heard her mother's voice behind her. "Laurel, you know we don't say 'shut up' in this family."

"But listen to her," Laurel cried. "She says she's skipping a grade!"

Laurel's mother gave Dr. Shade one of her meaningful looks.

"It's something we have to discuss. Jeanie's teacher sent a note home asking us to consider whether Jeanie should be placed a grade ahead. Your father and I will have to talk about it. I'm not sure it's a good idea," Mrs. Shade finished.

This was absolutely too much. How could it possibly be true? If it were true, why hadn't Jeanie said something about it before their father came home? And what teacher in her right mind would think Jeanie was ready for third grade? Why...

"She doesn't even know what fractions are!" Laurel burst out.

"Apparently she does," said her mother.

"How can she know how to read so well? She never told *me* she could. And where did she learn about fractions?"

Their mother bent down, smiling, and put her hands on Jeanie's shoulders. "Okay, kiddo, time to confess. Where did you get those reading skills? Where did you learn about fractions?"

A starburst smile spread across Jeanie's face. She pulled away from her mother and began spinning in circles and flapping her arms. "Where do you think?" she called as she spun. "On the *Learning* Channel, of course!"

"Oh, stop crowing," muttered Laurel.

"Why should I?" Jeanie answered, and let out an earsplitting imitation of a rooster's crow.

Among Jeanie's talents, which now appeared to include high-level reading and mathematics, was a gift for mimicry. She could copy the sound of a kitten mewing, a car engine starting, a microwave beeping. The noises were so realistic that if you closed your eyes, it was almost spooky. And this crowing sound, Laurel had to admit, was one of Jeanie's best.

For a minute Laurel found herself wishing that she could curl up into a little ball and join Nightshade under the sofa. She *should* be feeling proud for her sister. She was well aware of that—painfully aware. But the idea of Jeanie in third grade was just too much. It meant she would even be on the same playground as Laurel. The first and second graders, on the other hand, were safely tucked away in a separate lunchroom and on a separate playground.

And Jeanie reading at a high level! How long had that been going on? Laurel was supposed to be the big reader of the family.

Meet our daughter Jeanie, Laurel pictured her parents saying to an imaginary group. *You know she's gifted! And talented! And creative— this girl is so creative she actually has a television in her head! Oh, and here's Laurel. So solid. Our little… brick.*

As the girls got ready for bed that night, their parents' voices sounded in the family room. No doubt they were discussing Jeanie and her class placement. At first Laurel strained to hear, but she couldn't really make out the words. And somehow the effort of listening was making her feel worse—like a sneaky, eavesdropping brick. She turned out the light and lay back.

Through the half-open door Laurel saw Nightshade padding down the hallway, heading toward their room. She sprang out of bed and shut the door before Nightshade could slip inside.

Not tonight, Laurel thought. *Maybe I should be more generous. But if I have to watch Nightshade curl up on Jeanie's bed tonight, I just don't think I can take it.*

Morning light filtered into the bedroom as a breeze fluttered the curtains. Laurel's sheets felt smooth, and her pillow was scrunched just right. The temperature was perfect. Somewhere a ragged voice began singing, something about a hopeless yearning and rock 'n' roll.

The clock radio had gone off. Time to get up. Laurel moaned. She didn't want to move a single muscle.

She looked over at Jeanie's bed and was startled to see Jeanie staring back brightly. "How long have you been awake?" Laurel asked.

"How long have *you* been awake?" Jeanie answered in one of her voices designed to irritate. Then her face took on its usual serious expression. "Laurel, do you remember second grade?"

"Yes. Of course I remember."

"Did you *like* second grade?"

Laurel thought for a while. "Yes. Yes, I did. You know, I really loved it."

She tried to describe her memories to Jeanie. How the kids still sat at tables together. How every day brought some exciting new thing—soccer! chapter books! computer lab! How one time she had tried to see how far she could count, and realized she could count forever, and knew that she would be able to count forever forever.

"Were the kids nicer than they are in first grade?" Jeanie wanted to know.

Laurel wasn't sure how to respond. "I don't know. They were nice. Well, there was the time that Molly Wittmer and I had a huge fight." Laurel smiled.

"Tell me," Jeanie said.

"Oh, it was so… it was really so stupid…." Laurel chuckled to herself.

"Stop laughing and tell me!"

As Laurel described the scene, in her mind she could actually see the second-grade Molly Wittmer, plump cheeks and hair in bangs, sitting across from her at the table. She could see the radiators under the classroom windows and the streaks of crayon on the table in front of her.

Laurel had been busy with addition problems. Suddenly there was a loud *ka-choo* and a small splat. Across the table Molly Wittmer had let loose with a Mount Vesuvius of a sneeze, and Laurel was now staring at a blob of mucus that had landed near her hand. It was greenish and shaped something like a dolphin.

The second-grade Laurel had felt a wave of disgust. "Clean this thing away from my place," she had whispered to Molly.

"What thing?" Molly had whispered back.

"This *yucky* thing," Laurel had hissed. Molly pretended not to understand.

They had gone back and forth for a while that way, Laurel pointing angrily, Molly acting indignant. Meanwhile the greenish dolphin just glistened.

Laurel had narrowed her eyes at Molly Wittmer. Molly's cheeks weren't just plump, they were *fat.* And her nose, with its reddened, widened nostrils, was beginning to look like a pig snout. Molly was snuffling, and that had a piggish sound to it, too. *She is nothing but a fat pig,* the second-grade Laurel thought, *who won't budge out of her sty.*

The greenish dolphin thing was now spreading, settling in.

Laurel started to lose it. "Clean this thing," she hissed with such force that her throat hurt. *"Clean it clean it clean it!"*

Molly crossed her arms stubbornly. "I don't know what you're talking about."

"I'm talking about this yucky thing that came out of your nose," Laurel exclaimed. The startled class turned and stared. The students tittered. Then they roared with laughter. Molly and Laurel were never good friends again.

Jeanie looked so transfixed by this story that Laurel had to chuckle. "You know something funny that I remember? I remember being frustrated that I couldn't think of a polite word for the dolphin thing. All I could think was that 'booger' and 'snot' weren't polite."

"That's right. You know better than that, Laurel." Jeanie's voice was an obvious imitation of their mother's. "You know we don't say 'booger' and 'snot' in this family."

As usual, Jeanie didn't crack a smile. But Laurel burst out laughing. "I couldn't think of any other word, though! Maybe now I'd say 'nasal mucus,' that's polite. I think even Mom would let us say 'nasal mucus.'"

"So. Who cleaned up the green dolphin thing?"

"I did," Laurel said. "And it was *soooo* disgusting!"

Jeanie let out a horrified gasp. Finally her face spread into a wide grin, and she and Laurel began shaking with laughter.

"What on earth is going on in here?" Their mother was standing in the doorway. "Hurry up, you two. I'm making waffles."

The girls rushed to their kitchen barstools. As Jeanie climbed onto hers, she announced: "I do *not want* to skip second grade."

"What made you decide that?" her mother asked.

Jeanie scowled. "Just no."

Dr. Shade looked up from the paper and said, "I see WEGG really has a bee in its bonnet." In response to his wife's puzzled look, he added, "Westchester Ever Green Group."

Laurel burst in. "I almost forgot! There's a new boy in my class named Holyfield!"

Jeanie looked at Laurel, intent. "What's he like?"

"There's something creepy about him," Laurel said. "I think he has a twin sister in Shannon's class."

"I *knew* he'd be creepy," Jeanie said.

"Jeanie, we know you loved that tree," their mother said. "But listen—two points. First of all, we don't know for sure that all these Holyfields are the same family. And second, if I had done some very bad thing—would that make *you* creepy?"

Nightshade chose that moment to come rocketing into the kitchen. From her barstool perch, Jeanie started to reach down for him. Then she thought the better of it and straightened up.

"Two points," she said. "First, we never ever in our whole lives ever knew anyone named Holyfield before, so it almost has to be the same family. And second, Mom, you could *never* do some very bad thing, so I could never be creepy."

And no one said anything at all after that.

chapter 6

Why can't Laurel seem to keep her eyes off the Holyfield boy? There he is now, his lanky figure catching Laurel's eye as soon as she gets to school. He is sitting at the top of the steps by the main door, wearing loose khakis. Usually the steps are packed with students hanging out until the bell rings. Today they are deserted, except for him.

As Laurel watches him, she hears a voice in her ear. It is Chrissie Paradiso.

"Look at that Holyfield kid," Chrissie is saying. "I'm surprised he has the nerve to come to this school. My mom says it's the same thing as murder, them cutting down that tree like that. They come here from Pittsburgh or wherever and do a thing like that. She says the whole bunch should be strung up by their thumbs."

Laurel turns and looks into Chrissie's warm dark eyes. But in her mind she's picturing a family all dangling by their thumbs. It seems an odd way to punish someone. And how odd to hear such a grotesque proposal coming from gentle Chrissie. Does she get the same picture in her head that Laurel does? Or is she just repeating words?

★ ★ ★

Once in the classroom, Laurel watched the Holyfield boy out of the corner of her eye. His desk was in front of hers, one row to the right. Most of the time he looked straight ahead, so she couldn't see much of his face—just a length of lean jaw, partly covered by his floppy light brown hair.

But once in a while, when he turned to the left, she would catch a silvery greenish glint from his strange eyes. Then Laurel would shiver a little.

The boy never smiled. His face showed no expression at all.

"He's some kind of android," whispered Collin, whose desk was behind Laurel's. "Watch this."

Collin leaned forward and hissed.

"Tree killer."

Those words were so chilling. Laurel closed her eyes. Behind her, Collin hissed louder.

"Hey. *Tree killer.*"

Laurel opened her eyes again, just in time to see the boy's head turn. It turned exactly halfway around. The greenish gray eyes blinked once. Laurel felt a flickering sense of something about to open... but no. The face showed no change. Then the head turned back again.

"See what I mean?" Collin said into Laurel's ear. "He's an android from outer space." Collin's voice grew louder and more theatrical. "An android from the Tree-Killer Planet."

"Be quiet, Collin," Laurel whispered uneasily. Mrs. Gombiner was frowning in their direction. But something else was also making Laurel uneasy. It was something about the glee in Collin's voice. And something, too, about the lean face and wrist of the Holyfield boy.

The kids were each describing their summer, and it was Aubrey Madison's turn. Aubrey was athletic and superarticulate and rich. Her father was a famous jazz cellist who gave concerts all over the world—sometimes even on public television. She was the only African American student in Laurel's class. And she was also easily the most beautiful girl in the school. Aubrey Madison: sixth-grade icon.

Aubrey seemed to walk on some airy cushion just above the ground. When she smiled, her cheeks turned into two perfect globes, like the carved wooden balls on the legs of the Shades' leather armchair. She was serene and gracious and warm, and every girl in the class longed to be her friend. Yet Aubrey clearly lived on a higher plane. She probably hung out with Kennedys and Cosbys, people like that. She probably vacationed in Fiji. Aubrey Madison: girl of mystery and magic.

Aubrey went out for lunch every day. She always breezed into the building at the end of the lunch period, just as the bell was ringing. It had entered the sixth-grade vocabulary—arriving at the last possible minute was called "Aubrey Madison time." Aubrey Madison: standard-setter for cool.

So now Laurel strained to hear Aubrey's description of her summer. She wanted a glimpse, however remote, of this magical life.

"I had a pretty terrific summer," Aubrey was saying. The classroom fell silent.

"A little travel, a little tennis, and lots of... just plain fun!" Aubrey bestowed a radiant smile on the classroom. The students took in their breath. It was like watching an actress being interviewed at the Oscars.

An uncomfortable thought was creeping over Laurel. At first she'd just been stuck on what to say about her own summer. But now she was realizing that if all the kids had to talk about their summer, that meant the Holyfield boy would have to say something. They were going by rows, and it was nearly his turn.

Laurel's mind flooded with unpleasant pictures. In her imagination the boy was standing up and talking in a robot monotone. And the other students were all rising from their seats, hurling turquoise spitballs at the boy, shouting, "Tree killer, tree killer." The pale greenish gray eyes were blinking as the turquoise spitballs bounced off the boy's face.

Laurel's body jerked up and out of her seat. She rushed past a slightly surprised Mrs. Gombiner, mumbling, "Bathroom." Chrissie Paradiso, whose seat was near the door, gave her a look of exaggerated shock, but Laurel didn't care. She just could not watch what was about to happen.

Cutting down the climbing tree was terrible—it made Laurel sick. But she still had no stomach for seeing this boy humiliated. Was there some strange disconnection in her head? She could close her eyes and see the pitiful stump that used to be the climbing tree, and anger would rise up. But looking at this thin, solitary Holyfield boy... well, he seemed pitiful, too.

In the bathroom Laurel stood by the window and studied her nails. Then she thought, *What if someone from my class comes in and sees that I didn't really have to go?* She went into a bathroom stall and locked the door.

How many students sat between Aubrey Madison and the Holyfield boy? Three; no, four. How long would each student talk? Maybe a minute. Laurel counted to sixty, four times.

But what if they each took *two* minutes? Laurel polished her shoes with little wads of toilet paper that she dampened with her tongue. Surely the Holyfield boy must have finished by now.

In fact, when Laurel came back into the classroom, all the students were done. Laurel turned to Collin and whispered as quietly as she could, "What happened?"

Collin shrugged his shoulders. "What happened with what?"

That afternoon Mrs. Gombiner's students had computer lab. The school district was in the process of upgrading its technology, and

Tuckerman had replaced its computers over the summer. Now each student in computer lab had a brand-new computer with direct Internet access, a much bigger monitor, and a totally different operating system. These computers were much more advanced than the old ones, Mr. Schmitt, the computer instructor, kept saying.

But after a few minutes at one of the new computers, Laurel wanted to smash in its screen. She'd been fine on last year's equipment, and of course the computer at the Shades' house was a breeze. But this one was totally alien.

The mouse was a different design, for one thing, with fussier timing and more buttons to click. And the keyboard keys meant different things now, so nothing responded the way Laurel expected. The screen kept changing unexpectedly.

Laurel felt as though she were lost in a maze that went on forever and kept transforming itself. She fervently hoped that the rest of the class was struggling, too.

"At the end of this unit your document must contain at least five hundred words of text," Mr. Schmitt was reciting, "incorporating at least one graph or pie chart, at least two images from your clip art, one numerical table containing a minimum of three columns…"

His voice was reedy and tense. As the class went on, he pushed his glasses up on his nose more and more frequently, and he jerked his fingers through his hair so often it began to look like feathers.

It was Mr. Schmitt's first year at Tuckerman. His obvious discomfort made Laurel temporarily forget her own anxiety. Sometimes she secretly felt a little sorry for new teachers. This Mr. Schmitt, for example, was as awkward as… as what? Her mind began roaming. As awkward as a freshly hatched chick. A freshly hatched chick—yes.

My teacher hatched this morning.
His feathers are still wet.
If the teacher's just a little chick,
Can there be a teacher's pet?

When Laurel's mind returned to the classroom, she realized that Mr. Schmitt had been leaning over her shoulder watching her. For quite a while now. *Uh-oh. Am I the only one who's confused?* she suddenly wondered.

"Anything you don't understand?" he asked her.

Laurel felt so hopelessly lost she wanted to laugh at his question. But it came out sounding a little like a sob.

"Don't be frustrated," Mr. Schmitt said gently. "Of course it will take a while." His kindness was astonishing.

"Let's go one step at a time," he whispered. "Let me get you back to the main menu." His fingers tapped across Laurel's keyboard, and then she was staring at the opening screen. Mr. Schmitt guided her into the word-processing program. She began typing with confidence.

Suddenly her beautiful typing turned into a ridiculous narrow stripe of words running down the center of the screen. Laurel groaned.

"Do you know what happened?" asked Mr. Schmitt.

"Of course not," Laurel said, and then flushed at how sharp it sounded.

"You hit the control key instead of the shift key."

"I couldn't have," Laurel said. Then, looking more closely at the keyboard: "This keyboard is messed up! The control key is in the wrong place! Oh man, I really hate this new computer!"

"Well, the control key may be in a different place than you're used to," Mr. Schmitt said earnestly. "After a while, though, I think it will seem like the right place. And, Laurel, I'd like you to try and look at things a little differently. This is just a machine. It's a machine that operates on simple logic. It's not worth hating. Every piece of information it handles has to be broken down into a pattern of simple ons or offs. That's all a computer can deal with."

Logic, did he say? Simple on and off? What was he talking about? Not *this* magic box.

As Mr. Schmitt continued talking to Laurel, his manner grew livelier but more distant, as if he had begun lecturing to a large audience. "You need to try to get past the surface jazz and understand what's really going on with a computer. Forget the icons. Forget the sound effects and all that other stuff. All a computer is really doing is responding to the simplest possible commands: on, off. That's it—just on, off. Say, have you ever been to a Yankees game?"

Mr. Schmitt wasn't waiting for an answer. It turned out he wanted to talk about the Yankee scoreboard, the one that flashed pictures and messages to the crowd, like KISS IT GOOD-BYE. With great fervor, he explained that the scoreboard was made up of row upon row of small lightbulbs. To spell something out, the switch for each individual light was either turned on or left off. Each bulb became a tiny part of a large message. "You understand that much, right?" Mr. Schmitt asked Laurel eagerly. "Okay, now motion."

He continued. If each light were sent an on/off instruction several times a second, and the timing of all the light flashes were coordinated, an image on the scoreboard could appear to move. For example, the board could display the image of a huge baseball flying off the screen, losing its leather cover in the process. "You understand that much, right?" Mr. Schmitt asked again. Well, a computer did exactly the same thing. It just did it with tremendously more switches and tremendously faster pulses per second. But it still boiled down to just on or off.

Suddenly Mr. Schmitt was distracted. "Excuse me," he said to

Laurel. "I have to see what happened to this other student's screen."

He hurried over to where the Holyfield boy was sitting. The borders of his computer screen looked strange. They were filled with a three-dimensional, swirling, symmetrical pattern. It was like nothing Laurel had ever seen.

Mr. Schmitt watched in silence for a moment. Then Laurel heard him say, "Did you design your own wallpaper?" After the Holyfield boy nodded, Mr. Schmitt asked him, "How did you figure out how to animate it?"

The two huddled over the keyboard. A couple of other students moved over to watch.

Mr. Schmitt and the Holyfield boy were absorbed in the computer. They were creating fantastic surging images on the screen, one after another. More students drifted over.

Eventually the entire class stood behind them in a semicircle. They were speechless. Laurel felt as though she were watching a master organist in a cathedral creating exquisitely beautiful worlds with a touch of the keys. How strange that this boy of all people could create such delicate beauty.

Laurel would remember that awed semicircle later. She would remember it after the students had been dismissed. After they'd all found the PTA newsletter, *Knoll News,* in their cubbies. The newsletter mentioned that the town's next Conservation Board meeting would include a discussion of "recent incidents on the Chestnut Knoll Nature Trail." Everyone was encouraged to attend.

As they walked home from school, Shannon leaned in to Laurel conspiratorially. "What are you wearing to Felicity Osterman's party?"

Laurel wrinkled her forehead. She couldn't remember anything about a party for Felicity.

Shannon's eyes grew round. She clapped her hands over her mouth and looked horrified. Then she said, "Oops" and lightly slapped herself on the cheek. "Gosh, Laurel, I'm really sorry. I truly, truly am. I just assumed you were invited."

"That's okay." But in fact Laurel's stomach was not feeling all that okay.

"You know, that Felicity is really getting conceited, if you ask me," Shannon said. "I guess she thinks she's too cool for you now."

"Guess so." Laurel could scarcely believe that Felicity, who had seemed such a good friend for so long, would do this. Felicity Osterman, who was always laughing and who was addicted to cartwheels. Whom Laurel had known since kindergarten.

"I hear Aubrey's definitely going to the party," Shannon said.

Laurel started. This was very, very big news. Aubrey dipped down into their world only on rare and thrilling occasions. Laurel remembered a Halloween party the year before. Aubrey had arrived late, heart-stoppingly gorgeous. She was all in silver, wearing a beaded midriff top and low-slung shimmering harem pants. A silver chain clung to her lithe waist. She wore a transparent silver veil and glitter on her face.

In one hand Aubrey held what looked like a gold-and-silver teapot. It seemed handmade and ancient, like something from *The Arabian Nights*. Then everyone at the party seemed to breathe at once: "She's a genie! She's a genie from a magic lantern!"

Aubrey's genie costume won first place. But she herself had left, of course, long before the winner was announced.

Laurel really didn't feel like thinking about what Aubrey might wear to Felicity's.

"You know, I think it's really shocking that Felicity didn't invite you," Shannon offered. Laurel didn't answer, but Shannon continued. "I mean, I think it's really terrible. I mean, you always invite her to your parties."

If only Shannon would stop talking. Her sympathetic remarks somehow made Laurel feel worse. It was a relief when Shannon started squinting ahead and pointing. "There she is," she said.

"Who—Jeanie?" asked Laurel. Jeanie was once again walking home in front of them, a house and a half ahead.

"No! Duh. I'm talking about that Holyfield girl. Ahead of Jeanie."

Looking farther ahead, Laurel saw a small girl with a dark ponytail down her back. She was walking next to a tall lanky boy whose back Laurel was beginning to know well. From this angle something about the loose drape of his khakis and the way his longish light brown hair was falling made Laurel think of an explorer just back from a safari.

"Did I tell you that Holyfield kid's named Roberta?" Shannon said. "Wouldn't you know she'd have a dorky name like that. It sounds like a prune or something."

Laurel's favorite aunt was named Roberta, so the name did not sound dorky or prunelike to her. She had always liked the name. She had even named her favorite teddy bear Roberta. Well, no need to share that with Shannon.

The street was usually overflowing with Tuckerman kids that time of day. The grass was worn away for several feet on either side of the sidewalk. But now, around the Holyfields, the street was deserted. They might just as well have been walking on the moon.

That was when Laurel thought back to the Holyfield boy at his computer, and how the whole class had stood behind him in an awed semicircle.

Shannon was now hanging on her arm and giggling. Once again she was making the pig snort of yesterday. Laurel tried to laugh, too, but it somehow didn't seem as funny today.

She felt weary. She was glad when she and Jeanie got to their house.

There on the piano was an envelope for Laurel. In it was an invitation to Felicity Osterman's party.

★ ★ ★

On Friday nights the Shades usually had pizza delivered and rented a video. This week was Jeanie's turn to pick the movie, and she had chosen to watch *Aladdin* for the hundredth time. She and Laurel lay on the floor of the family room with fat cushions under their heads, munching microwave popcorn. Their parents were sprawled on the sofa.

Jeanie rolled over next to Laurel and propped her chin up on her elbows. "Laurel. Ask me what my three wishes would be if I had a genie."

"Fine. What."

"Not like that. Ask me the right way."

Laurel didn't feel like arguing, so she just sighed. "Okay, so if you had a genie, what would your three wishes be?"

"My first wish would be that the climbing tree would come back again."

Laurel heard a tiny catch in Jeanie's voice and felt a pang.

Then Laurel asked, as gently as possible, "What else would you wish for?"

"Nothing," Jeanie answered quietly.

"Huh?"

"I wouldn't ask for anything. I'd never use up my other two wishes so the genie would have to hang around me and be my friend forever."

Laurel felt another small pang. What could she say in response?

In the middle of the night Laurel was awakened by an unusual plinking sound. Sort of a plinking, sort of a ticking. What on earth could it be? It seemed to be coming from Jeanie's bed.

Once Laurel got used to the darkness, she could just see Nightshade. He was stretched on his side on Jeanie's bed. He was reaching up over his head, and his furry little tummy was arched out, so that his body formed a semicircle. He was plucking carefully at the threads of Jeanie's bedspread, like a tiny harpist.

Laurel was certain that when they had gone to bed, she had deliberately closed the door before Nightshade could get in. She turned and looked at their bedroom door. It was closed again now.

Boy, that Jeanie is really sneaky! Laurel thought. *She must have waited for me to fall asleep and then gotten Nightshade. And then shut the door to make sure he'd stay with her.*

Laurel picked Nightshade up from Jeanie's bed, so carefully she hardly breathed. He gave a small squeak but didn't squirm. He felt feather-light and silky. Laurel's heart swelled.

She placed him on her bed. He promptly jumped to the floor. Laurel's heart ached.

Laurel slithered to the floor and once again gathered Nightshade in her arms. She tiptoed to the door and down to the family room.

Laurel had planned to put Nightshade on the sofa. But now, here, in the empty, moonlit family room, it seemed cruel to deprive him of company. Instead, she carried him to her parents' room and placed him on their bed. She closed the door and tiptoed back to her room.

She lay with her eyes open for a long time. She was troubled. Had she just done something selfish? Was she being mean to Nightshade? Should she just let him stay on her sister's bed?

But there were two sisters, after all, and only one kitten. Wouldn't the fairest thing be for neither sister to sleep with the kitten? And Nightshade was supposed to have been a sort of birthday present for Laurel, after all. And he should be just as happy to sleep in their parents' bed. Surely this was the best way. When you thought about it.

Right?

chapter 7

Ah, Saturday morning! Comfortable pillows. Sun filling the room. Kitten curled up in a patch of sun on Jeanie's bed.

Laurel shoots straight up in bed.

"*Jeanie!* Jeanie—wake up right this second. How dare you go kidnap Nightshade?"

"Huh?" Jeanie says sleepily. Then, after blinking a few times: "What are you talking about? I didn't kidnap anyone!"

"You kidnapped Nightshade—you went and stole him for your bed!"

"I did not! He just came here by himself!"

"Stop lying to me—I *know* you did."

One of Jeanie's many amazing sound effects is a shriek so loud and high-pitched it makes Laurel's ears feel like the bristles of some tiny toothbrush are whirling madly inside them. That's the shriek Jeanie uses now.

"*I am not lying! I can't help it if he likes me better than you!*"

Laurel sprints down to their parents' room, propelled by fury. Jeanie is following so close behind she almost knocks Laurel over.

Mrs. Shade squints at the two of them from the bed. "Stop

fighting," she mumbles. "Go back to your room and stop fighting." She pulls the blankets over her head.

Jeanie jumps onto the bed. She pulls the blankets down again. "Listen, Mom, listen! Laurel called me a liar! Wake up!"

"Please get off the bed," their mother says sleepily. "And stop fighting."

"Mom, please listen, please." Laurel's voice is urgent. "Jeanie keeps stealing Nightshade to sleep with her, and she won't even admit it, and he was supposed to be for my birthday and everything. Jeanie, Mom told you to *get off the bed*!"

Now Mrs. Shade sits up. Her eyes are icy. "Quiet. Both of you," she says. "Just stop all this nonsense immediately or I will not take you into the city."

Then Laurel remembers. They are supposed to go shopping in New York City today. She gives Jeanie one last reproachful look. They trudge back up to their room and dress in silence.

They took the train into New York City—the city, everyone called it.

Laurel loved the train. Something about the rickety motion set her mind free. Sometimes it seemed to make her sad, but a good kind of sad, the kind of sad that she thought poets must feel.

She took out her wallet, which had a tiny pad and pencil inside, and began to write.

> *Different faces, different lives,*
> *Teenagers, old people, husbands and wives.*
> *We don't talk together, we don't look up.*
> *But we're all on one train with the same last stop.*

She stopped and thought. What was this poem really about? Ah, wait a minute.

> *Where are we going? What's the ride for?*
> *Who knows? The main thing is to hop on board!*

She smiled to herself. In all honesty, it sounded very good. And she hadn't even known what it was about!

The Fordham stop. One Hundred Twenty-fifth Street. They were practically at Grand Central Station.

Mrs. Shade called over to Jeanie, who was sitting across the aisle. Jeanie looked up, startled.

"I didn't mean to interrupt anything," Mrs. Shade said with a smile.

"That's okay, it's not important. It's just some stupid Skunky and Splat show. It must be a rerun, because here it is September and they've got all these jokes about the Easter Bunny."

A moment later they stepped off the train into Grand Central, and the metallic hot rush of the station surrounded them.

The shopping part of the trip was a total bust. When they emerged onto Forty-second Street, it was raining. Most of the streets seemed to be blocked off. Traffic was a hopeless honking tangle. The President was in town, it turned out.

"I wish the President would do something really good for New York City," Mrs. Shade sputtered, "like never come visit again!"

The Shades tried to get a taxi, then gave up. Laurel wanted to take the subway, but her mother said firmly, "I *cannot* handle the subway today." So they had hot chocolate and french fries at a deli just a few blocks from Grand Central, then decided to head back to Chestnut Knoll.

On the walk back to the station, the rain started sheeting down, and they took refuge in the lobby of an electronics company. *There's a Cyborg in Your Future . . . YOU!* said an eye-catching electronic display.

The electronic display was part of an exhibit demonstrating that Mind was about to merge with Machine. The exhibit's organizers claimed that the human race was morphing into something part flesh, part electronic circuitry—a race of "cyborgs."

The displays showed that if trends continued, computers would soon match the memory capacity of the human brain. They already far surpassed the brain in speed. And *neural nets* were being developed—computer structures that mimicked the workings of the brain, making a computer's "thinking" more human, and actually able to improve itself over time.

While machines became more like human beings, humans were becoming more machinelike. The exhibits showed amazing and real "wearable electronics": bracelets that were actually scanners or phones; eyeglasses with wireless Internet hookups and tiny screens.

The next step was implants: electronic devices actually implanted in the body. Science had already started down this road with things like pacemakers to regulate heartbeat and implants to correct hearing. The future would see a thousand times more corrective implants like these, some directly connected to the nervous system.

And in time implanted computer chips would expand normal human capabilities. Instant foreign-language translators and high-speed calculators, for example, would be imbedded in the brain.

Most of the people at the exhibit seemed excited about humanity's cyborg future. But Laurel found it vaguely unsettling.

On the way back the train was crowded and steamy. Laurel and Jeanie sat facing each other next to a window. Their mother sat several rows back.

Laurel's mind kept returning to the computer exhibit. *There's a Cyborg in Your Future…YOU!* Why was that so disturbing? It made Laurel think of the creepiest part in *Pinocchio,* when the bad boys were only *partly* turned into donkeys.... Or that strange fairy tale about seven brothers turned into swans. Their sister turned them back into humans by knitting magic sweaters, but she ran out of time and one brother was left forever with a swan wing for an arm. There was something sad and terrifying, Laurel thought, about being almost human but *not quite*. It seemed the worst fate of all—to not quite belong in any world.

She pulled out her notepad and reread the poem she'd written earlier. It now seemed remarkably stupid.

That evening Jeanie disappeared out back. Laurel followed her down to the place where the climbing tree had been.

Jeanie was standing with her back to the empty spot. She was staring at the Holyfield house.

Right now, in the twilight, the house had a desolate look. Just one window had a light in it, a small window on the ground floor, and somehow that solitary lighted window made the house look sadder than if it had been completely dark.

He is probably inside there right now, Laurel thought. There was no way he could be at a friend's house. Who would be his friend?

Laurel pictured that lean face, those unreadable silvery eyes, that prominent wrist bone.

Laurel thought about his breathtaking computer creations. She thought about the Holyfield brother and sister making their solitary way home. And then the damp twilight was bringing up a picture of the climbing tree: *That tree took me to Zanzibar / And other places strange and far / And to a special star way up in the sky....* Now a stinging, twisting, almost-crying feeling was building inside her, and Laurel wasn't sure exactly why.

chapter 8

On Monday morning a drawing waits on the Holyfield boy's chair. Laurel can see it from her seat. It is a drawing of a cut-down tree, with blood pouring out the trunk.

He comes in just ahead of Aubrey Madison and her last-minute cloud of radiance. Laurel's chest tightens.

He stops and stands perfectly still when he reaches his seat. There is a tiny twitch around his jawbone. Then he picks up the drawing, puts it inside his desk, and sits down.

The Holyfield boy shuts his eyes. They stay closed for several seconds. Suddenly—briefly, confusingly—Laurel yearns to put an arm around his shoulder. But then his eyes open again, and they have their usual unreadable look.

Laurel twists in her seat toward Collin. "Who did that?" she whispers.

"How should I know? I'm innocent." Then Collin flutters his lashes. "For a change." He smiles angelically.

Laurel does not feel like smiling. She feels troubled. She steals another glance at that lean face, that long, arched nose.

★ ★ ★

"Quiet now, everyone," Mrs. Gombiner was saying with a sharp glance in Laurel and Collin's direction. Then she beamed. "I have an announcement. I am delighted to announce that next Tuesday afternoon we'll be having a special assembly. The Grammy-winning musician Marlowe Madison has agreed to do a presentation for us on the history of jazz. In this town, of course, Marlowe Madison might be even better known as Aubrey Madison's father."

The announcement raised an excited buzz, and of course all heads turned toward Aubrey, who looked down modestly. Then she began to smile. It was a smile that unfolded slowly, like a sky-rocket traveling upward, then blossoming into a fireworks bouquet that filled the whole night sky.

That skyrocket smile jogged something in Laurel—not quite a memory, a fragment of a memory. It was a kind of mental snapshot of Aubrey Madison, talking with... Yuriko! Laurel could briefly see them in her mind: two dark heads of hair, one glossy-straight, the other a dark cloud, leaning together cozily next to the cubbies—and then Aubrey smiling a modest smile that slowly blazed into fireworks. Laurel couldn't seem to pull up any other fragments, but she took some comfort in this little piece of memory. Maybe Yuriko *had* had another friend after all. Maybe she'd been friends with none other than Aubrey Madison.

The last part of the day was computer lab. Laurel strode in lightheartedly. Then she sat down at the computer, turned it on, and was lost in the maze all over again.

For crying out loud, where *were* those commands for inserting charts and graphics? They seemed to have been relocated. And why did the information in her table keep going down the page instead of across?

Worst of all, today Laurel could not get rid of the suspicion that no one else was quite as lost as she was. Most of the class seemed to be clicking and punching the keyboard with gusto.

Mr. Schmitt came over and watched Laurel. Her brain began dumping its contents. The longer he stayed, the less she knew.

Mr. Schmitt gave her a nervous smile. Laurel's stomach clenched.

"I wonder if maybe David could help you," Mr. Schmitt said gently.

Who was David? Laurel wondered. But in almost the same instant she remembered the name of the Holyfield boy. David Holyfield.

She looked at Mr. Schmitt, feeling a little numb. He was conferring with the boy. She heard Mr. Schmitt saying something about showing her the difference between columns and tables. Then a chair was pulled up next to hers, practically touching hers, and the Holyfield boy sat in the chair.

Laurel wondered if there was any possibility that she might breathe in the same air that he breathed out. She knew that used air, carbon dioxide, was poisonous. But hadn't she heard that if there was any unused air around at all, your nose would find it and breathe it first?

He stretched his hands over Laurel's keyboard. Laurel watched his wrist. That prominent wrist bone looked like it was carved of ivory. If she touched it, would he notice?

Then Laurel watched his long fingers on the keyboard. They hardly seemed to move. They just rippled.

Laurel seemed to be having trouble breathing normally. Maybe it was carbon dioxide.

She really should be concentrating on the computer.

What the Holyfield boy could do with that keyboard was staggering. Laurel wordlessly watched him create magic. It was so far beyond anything she'd ever seen. She could not begin to follow the sequence of his computer maneuvers.

"How did you get so good?" Laurel finally breathed. Those were the first words either had spoken.

A silence.

Finally he answered. "My father."

Laurel flashed back to the cut-down tree, how it had looked the first time she saw it. Then an image of the bleeding-tree drawing pushed into her head.

Leave him alone, she scolded herself. *Back off!* But she couldn't seem to stop herself.

"What does your father do?" she asked.

After a moment of staring at his profile in silence, Laurel thought, *Maybe he's just not going to answer me.* She was aware of his swallowing and felt vaguely intrusive.

"He's a software developer," he finally said. His eyes stayed fixed on the monitor.

Then neither of them said anything. Laurel wished he would look right at her. She wanted to see his odd eyes—so hard to read, yet somehow so intense. At the same time, though, even imagining him looking at her brought on a wave of shyness.

The boy was totally absorbed in his computer conjuring. After about a minute of tables and columns, he seemed to have forgotten all about helping Laurel. Now it looked like he was designing a Web page. He was combining text with moving images he'd somehow created. The way he manipulated the keyboard was astonishing.

"You've got the magic touch with that computer," Laurel said after a while. She hadn't wanted to say it. It was stupid. But out it had popped. Why couldn't she seem to control herself?

The Holyfield boy turned and really looked at Laurel for the first time that day. His eyes—his strange, unreadable eyes—fixed on her like laser beams.

"In a sense," he said carefully, "the computer is part of me."

In a sense the computer is part of me?

Laurel looked into the green-gray eyes and felt an odd tingle. "What do you mean?"

But the bell was already ringing and the students were standing up. Without another word, the Holyfield boy gathered up his things and left.

The computer was part of him! What on earth could that mean? Laurel was wondering all the way home. She couldn't get the question out of her mind.

"You seem kinda strange today," Shannon said.

"I'm okay."

"Well, I guess I'd be feeling a little weird, too, if they made me sit practically in that Holyfield kid's lap! I heard about that." Shannon's eyes were wide and expectant.

Laurel vaguely wondered how the news could have reached Shannon so fast. But there were no words in her head to satisfy Shannon's obvious thirst for information.

"Are you sure nothing's wrong?" Shannon prodded.

"I'm okay. Nothing's wrong," Laurel said. But she wasn't even sure anymore if it was true. Something was certainly peculiar.

She couldn't seem to control her brain.

Not control her brain! Laurel caught herself. It sounded like something Jeanie might say. *"My brain isn't letting me watch the channel I want,"* she imagined Jeanie saying. Then she laughed out loud at this imaginary conversation.

"Why are you laughing?" Shannon demanded.

Laurel could not force any words out. She just wrinkled her forehead and shrugged her shoulders.

"Yeah right, you're really okay," Shannon said with a crooked smile. "If you say so."

Laurel jerked away from Shannon. She started running, running hard.

She hadn't even known she was going to do it. Her body had just started doing it before Laurel even realized. It was more of this out-of-control thing.

In a minute Laurel had caught up to Jeanie, who was the usual house and a half in front. Jeanie looked up at her and lifted her eyebrows a little. There was something oddly grown-up about the look on her face.

"Wait up," Laurel panted, feeling a rush of affection for her sister.

chapter 9

"I've just discovered this new channel on my television—a foreign-language channel," Jeanie is saying at breakfast. "And they're teaching a language that hardly anyone knows anymore. It's called Turbish. They spoke it in America before Columbus came."

This comment stirs Laurel's curiosity. She'd loved her fifth-grade unit on American Indians and even learned some words in Navajo. Besides, she has vowed to appreciate Jeanie more.

"So you're learning a Native American language?" Laurel asks enthusiastically.

"*Native American?* No, way before that," Jeanie scoffs. "These are the people who lived in America *before* the Native Americans."

Laurel feels her cheek muscles tighten. Her teeth are starting to clench.

"Anyway, in Turbish, the word for food is *pote,*" Jeanie says. "Spoon is *ammapote.* And the word for mother, let me think for a second... no, don't tell me.... Anyway, from now on I'm talking in Turbish *all the time.*"

All the time. Oh terrific. *Why* does Jeanie have to do this?

Why does she have to make it so hard to be nice to her? Why does she have to be so darn… Jeanie-ish?

I am putting a stop to this wacko language thing right now, Laurel resolves.

As soon as Mrs. Shade leaves the kitchen, Laurel leans toward Jeanie, whose fingers are busy fighting with one another. "Look at me," Laurel whispers, and Jeanie looks up.

"Now listen," Laurel continues in a low voice. "I want you to understand me. If you start talking in that weird language all the time, that's *it*. Do you hear me?"

"It's not a weird language, it's Turbish," Jeanie says placidly.

A hiss escapes through Laurel's clenched teeth. "I'm serious, Jeanie. If you keep doing this weird Turbish thing, I'm just not going to even talk to you. You will be *completely alone.*"

Jeanie just lifts her eyebrows a little. But her fingers have stopped fighting one another.

"By the way, Laurel," their mother said from the doorway, "I don't think you saw the letter you got yesterday." She handed Laurel a light brown envelope half-covered with postage stamps.

Laurel studied the envelope. In a box on the left side was a complicated string of words and numbers ending with the word JAPAN.

Laurel tore the letter open. *To my friend Laurel,* it began:

> Hello, it is me, Yuriko. Now I am in my Japanese town, called Denenchofu. Like Chestnut Knoll, it is not big but it is close to a big city, Tokyo. I am sorry I could not say good-bye to you when we go back to Japan, because it was very fast.
>
> I am happy for spending one year in America and *very* sad to leave. I hoped to stay longer. My family hoped to stay longer, but my father's company say no, he must come back. My friends here say I am sounding American! I say, no, in

America I am not sounding American! Now I must work hard to learn the Japanese things my friends study last year.

I am hoping you will send me some English soon, or I will forget it. I would be sad to forget! Please, write me an answer soon.

My father is laughing that I am sending "snail mail," but the Tuckerman School Directory has no e-mail address, so please, send me your e-mail address. Also, please, do you know the address of Aubrey Madison? It is not in the Tuckerman School Directory.

I am very happy for getting to know you. You are kind. You are the good thing of America.

Sincerely yours,
Yuriko

Laurel read the letter four times. She had never gotten a letter from another country before. She thought the envelope had a hint of an exotic smell. She would have to ask her mother to sniff it. Mrs. Shade had one of the most powerful noses in the world.

Yuriko had been just fine! Yuriko had been "happy" in America and "*very* sad" to leave. She'd had friends—friends like Aubrey Madison! *I guess I blew that whole thing out of proportion,* Laurel said to herself.

As she walked to school, Laurel thought about how Yuriko had complimented her. "You are kind," Yuriko had said, and "You are the good thing of America."

Laurel felt touched. But she didn't really deserve such praise. She cringed at the memory of her breakfast threats to Jeanie. Pretty poor stuff, from someone who was supposed to be the good thing of America.

★ ★ ★

Tuckerman School was starting its annual fitness campaign. The halls were filled with posters the third graders had made, all about healthy eating and exercise. In gym class each grade was being tested for fitness and then establishing fitness goals.

Aubrey Madison had been the brightest star of last year's campaign. She had taken first place in nearly every event for girls on their grade level. And she had climbed the rope to the gym ceiling in a record eight seconds, faster than any Tuckerman student, even the older grades.

Someone had snapped her picture at the top, one arm coiled around the rope, the other held up in a joyful sweep. Her hair radiated out like a glorious black halo. The photo ended up on the cover of the school-district calendar, the one sent to every home in Chestnut Knoll.

During the fitness campaign the boys were split from the girls for gym class, and Mrs. Gombiner's girls had gym with the girls from Ms. Scherer's class. Mrs. Turk, the gym teacher, was putting the girls in pairs to help each other do calisthenics.

This first time was going to be awkward for Laurel. Shannon was in Ms. Scherer's class. It had been two days since that walk home from school when Laurel had broken away and run ahead. She hadn't seen Shannon since then. She wasn't sure what to say to her. There wasn't exactly an argument to patch up. There was just an awkwardness.

Then Laurel heard Shannon talking to Mrs. Turk, sounding upset.

"I shouldn't have to be partners with someone I don't want to," Shannon was saying. "I should be able to pick who my partner is, what with the property taxes we pay."

Laurel edged closer. She saw the Holyfield girl standing next to Shannon. This was the first time Laurel had seen her from the front.

She was tiny; tiny and fragile-looking. Her dark hair was in a long, low ponytail. She wore gold-framed glasses. Her skin looked tan. Her teeth were very white and somewhat large; they looked perfect, Laurel observed. She had high, round, carved-looking cheeks—though not as round and carved-looking as Aubrey Madison's, of course.

Mrs. Turk's rosy face looked troubled.

"I'm not going to argue with you about this, Shannon," she said. Then her eyes landed on Laurel.

"Do you have a partner yet?" Mrs. Turk sounded anxious. "Look, Laurel, I'd like you to be Roberta's partner."

Why me? were the first words to fly into Laurel's head. This was plainly unfair. This was outrageous, really, being forced to pair up with one of Shannon's castoffs.

Chrissie Paradiso caught Laurel's eye and made a horrified expression.

Then Yuriko's words were in Laurel's head. *You are kind. You are the good thing of America.*

Am I really the good thing of America? Laurel again thought about her pettiness at breakfast. She also remembered that time at Cleve's when she learned Yuriko had gone back to Japan. She'd then seen in a flash how far she fell short of being a really good person.

But she had hoped for a second chance.

Of course, this Holyfield girl was not like Yuriko. She wasn't from another country or anything like that. It was a whole different situation.

But hey, let's face it, Mrs. Turk would probably make Laurel be this kid's partner whether she wanted to or not. What was the point in stalling?

Laurel took a deep breath. "Okay, come on," she said. "I've already got a mat."

And as she turned around, Laurel didn't notice the look of relief on Mrs. Turk's face, the look of sympathy on Chrissie's, or the look of amusement on Shannon's.

Belatedly she did notice Aubrey Madison. Apparently Aubrey had been approaching her and Roberta. Laurel's heart picked up speed. Aubrey had wanted to be her partner!

But now it was too late. Mrs. Turk was asking Aubrey to help her demonstrate the exercises.

Oh man! The chance of a lifetime, gone. Laurel would have been the envy of the school.

In spite of her fragile appearance, Roberta turned out to be very good at calisthenics. She bobbed up and down doing sit-ups while Laurel held her feet.

Suddenly Laurel was imagining the brother there doing sit-ups while she held his feet. She batted the thought away. *Don't think about him. And definitely don't talk about him.*

Laurel studied Roberta's eyes behind the glasses. They were basic brown—not like her brother's strange silvery green ones.

Laurel suddenly heard her own voice sounding in her ears. "Your brother is in my class."

Rats! *Why* had she said that?

Roberta just smiled a little, breathing hard.

"You know, he's amazing on the computer." Now the words were just rushing out of Laurel's mouth. "He said something to me in our computer class that I didn't understand, though. Something about the computer being part of him. 'In a sense the computer is part of me'—that's what he said."

Laurel stopped talking as she saw the strange look on Roberta's face.

Roberta abruptly stopped doing sit-ups. She sat forward and put her hand on Laurel's arm, which was holding Roberta's feet down. The look in Roberta's eyes was almost pleading. She spoke in a low voice.

"That is not really my brother."

Laurel decided she must not have heard correctly. "That isn't really your brother?" She searched Roberta's face. But Roberta wasn't saying anything more, not that day.

chapter 10

Laurel keeps turning the puzzle pieces around in her mind, over and over, but they won't fit. It's making her crazy. *In a sense the computer is part of me.* And *That is not really my brother.*

In a sense the computer *is* part of him. And he is not really her *brother.*

As Laurel reshuffles these baffling comments, she keeps picturing those unreadable eyes, that face that shows no feelings. She keeps thinking about the almost supernatural talent with computers. She remembers Collin's remark: *"He's some kind of android."*

His father is a software developer, he had said so—but he clearly hadn't wanted to talk about it.

And one more piece, the oldest piece, an almost forgotten piece: the time she and Jeanie had first gone to the Holyfield house. When Jeanie had spied and reported back. There was a girl inside, Jeanie had said. It must have been Roberta. Jeanie had said the girl was staring sadly into the computer monitor, as if looking for something she'd lost. Jeanie had come away convinced that something was lost inside the computer.

These are the pieces of the Holyfield puzzle, the pieces that won't fit together. One thing is emerging, though: computers are there at every turn. Computers are at the heart of the mystery. But how?

And how do these pieces fit with the climbing tree? Why would the Holyfields want to cut it down? Just for the extra light and space? Or were they bothered by the way it drew kids near their house? And Roberta seems so fragile somehow. Is she afraid of something?

It was enough to make you crazy, all right. Good thing Laurel wasn't walking home with Shannon.

Shannon had surprised her after gym class. Instead of acting uncomfortable or standoffish, she had gushed all over Laurel. As soon as the class headed out of the gym, Shannon had hurried over to Laurel, almost shoving other girls aside.

Shannon had grabbed Laurel's shoulder. "How's it going?" Without waiting for an answer, she had continued. "I have to ask you something. Why don't you meet me at my classroom after school so we can walk home together? I've got something to do that'll just take me about a sec."

Laurel had said yes. After school she had gathered up Jeanie, and the two of them had waited for Shannon outside Ms. Scherer's room. As it turned out, they had waited quite a while. Shannon was apparently involved in some after-school club.

Laurel had looked at her sister's forlorn expression and felt bad. This was so unfair to Jeanie, really: the poor kid had nothing to do, nothing but stand around and wait.

Then Jeanie had started slapping the sides of the hallway cubbies rhythmically, as if she were playing a gigantic set of drums. Soon she'd added an upturned trash can to the arrangement.

Laurel had started to feel embarrassed. "Stop it, Jeanie," she had whispered.

"This is a very rare drumbeat language," Jeanie had answered. "They just did a special on it on my foreign-language channel."

Laurel's embarrassment had flashed into anger. "Could you please shut up about your stupid television," she had snapped.

Jeanie had snapped back, in her Mrs. Shade imitation, "You know we don't say 'shut up' in this family."

Laurel had clenched her teeth, hard. Then she had caught Shannon's eye. "I'll catch you later," Laurel had mouthed.

But Shannon, inside the classroom, had shaken her head violently from side to side. "Just another minute! I swear!" she'd called.

Many more minutes went by. Jeanie had lain down flat on her back in the hallway and flailed her arms and legs against the floor.

"I'm making a dust angel," she had explained. For a split second Laurel pictured her fingers wrapped around Jeanie's throat.

A group of fifth-grade boys walking down the hall had stopped. They stared, first at the spread-eagled Jeanie, then at Laurel. *This is foolish*, Laurel thought. *I'm a fool.*

With new resolve, she had waved good-bye to Shannon and turned around.

"No, wait! I'm almost ready!" Shannon had insisted, but Laurel had continued walking down the hall.

She had been startled when Shannon seemed almost to fly up from behind her and grab her arm.

"Just wait one sec, Laurel! I've got to ask you something."

Shannon then pulled her to the side of the hall and cupped her hand around Laurel's ear. She began talking in a whisper so hot and forceful that Laurel's ear buzzed. "What were you talking about?" Then, in response to Laurel's puzzled look: "You know, you and that Holyfield girl!"

Anger and hurt had flared through Laurel. *This* was Shannon's urgent question? She had wasted Laurel's time for this—this petty gossip? Didn't Shannon respect her at all? But then Laurel was feeling just as angry at herself. *You're the one who hung around and hung around and wasted your own time,* she thought. *Congratulations. You've just proved yourself a major fool.*

But these feelings were way too raw and complicated to show to Shannon. So Laurel had made her face as blank as possible. "Shannon, it wasn't anything," she'd simply said. "We really have to leave now." That time she didn't look back. She'd been fool enough for one day.

And that's how she'd ended up walking home with Jeanie. For a change, the two of them were actually walking side by side, instead of Jeanie being a house and a half ahead. But Jeanie seemed busy with her television—"so many cooking shows this time of day!" Laurel heard her mumble. So Laurel could absorb herself in the puzzle of the Holyfield boy.

When they got home, Marina, the cleaning woman, was busy in the study. Marina came every other Thursday, and Laurel was fascinated by her. Marina spoke mostly Polish—but her eyes! There was a whole warm world in there. Laurel flopped into the leather armchair near Marina.

Marina was vigorously dusting the pictures on the mantel. She held up one of Jeanie and Laurel, about ages four and eight, wearing lacy party dresses.

"Very nice," Marina said. "Very nice." When Marina did use any English words, she generally repeated them for good measure.

Laurel looked at the photo. She had always secretly disliked it. She remembered when it was taken. The photographer had struggled for a long time to set up a large cloudy-looking screen behind the girls. While he battled the screen, Jeanie kept flipping up Laurel's lace sleeve, and Laurel kept smoothing it back down.

When the photographer finally began snapping pictures,

Laurel felt as though she were experiencing space travel. There was an intensely bright light in her eyes. A buzzing filled the room, interrupted by the commands of the photographer: "Chin up, sugar!" and "Over this way!" But Laurel couldn't see the photographer anymore. All she could see was the buzzing brightness.

The proofs arrived a week later. In every single one, the sleeve of Laurel's dress was flipped up at a ridiculous angle. And now it was forever framed that way. Laurel's sleeve was flipped up for all eternity.

Just now Marina was leaning over and putting one hand on Laurel's shoulder, a compassionate look in her eyes. "Sad?" she asked, although at first Laurel thought she'd said, "Sod?"

"No, not sod," Laurel answered.

She hadn't wanted to say "sad" the usual American way, because it might sound like she was correcting Marina. But now, as Laurel heard herself saying "sod," it almost sounded as though she were making fun of Marina.

"I'm not unhappy," she continued hastily. "Just thinking."

Marina smiled and shrugged at the same time, the way she did when she didn't understand. Laurel gave her what she hoped was a reassuring smile. "Everything's fine."

Marina clucked her tongue. Then she held up a paper and shook her head sadly. To Laurel's surprise, it was that article about Amur cork trees. She'd forgotten to ask her mom about it.

Marina's fingertip brushed across the photo of the cork tree. "Before, I walk past tree every day. Poor *vee-vyur-ka*"—or that was what it sounded like she said. "No more home for… *vee-vyur-ka*."

This comment, half-English, half-Polish, thoroughly baffled Laurel. *"Vee-vyur-ka?"* she repeated, searching Marina's face for clues.

"*Vee-vyur-ka,* this means…" Marina looked perplexed, but for just a moment. Then she bent down low and spread her hand out. She fluttered her fingers, from the floor to over her head.

"Butterfly?" Laurel speculated.

"No, no." Marina laughed. She thought for a minute. Then her face lit up. She cleared her throat importantly. *"Ska-VIRL,"* she said, beaming.

What on earth was Marina saying?

"Ska-VIRL. Vee-vyur-ka, this means *ska-VIRL."*

Ska-VIRL, ska-VIRL. The sounds kept repeating in Laurel's head until they slid into place. *"SQUIRREL!"* she shouted triumphantly.

Vee-vyur-ka meant *squirrel.* So a home for *vee-vyur-ka* was a home for squirrels. That's what Marina had to say about the climbing tree being cut down: no more home for squirrels.

After this first thrill of understanding, though, Laurel felt puzzled all over again. Yes, the climbing tree was gone. But the squirrels still had lots of other homes, didn't they? Surely one tree home was much like another to a squirrel. In fact, from a squirrel's point of view, wasn't the whole nature trail just one home after another?

What exactly do you mean when you say *no more* home for squirrels? Laurel wanted to ask. Then she thought about how to put this question into words for Marina and suddenly felt exhausted. Enough for one day.

Laurel sank back in her chair. The Holyfield boy came flickering into her mind. She imagined him sitting on the arm of the chair, right next to her.

She tried to reconstruct their conversation in computer class word for word. *"In a sense the computer is part of me"* were the words that kept returning to her mind.

Laurel sighed. If only she and Marina really spoke a common language. Laurel felt certain that Marina would give good advice. She could see the understanding in her eyes.

The Holyfields had all the missing puzzle pieces, of course. Was there some delicate way to ask Roberta?

★ ★ ★

Laurel hurried over to her at the start of gym the next day. Roberta was already stretching on a mat, legs spread wide, forehead touching the floor. Her dark hair fanned out around her.

"Do you want to be my partner?" Laurel asked.

Roberta looked up shyly. She moved her legs back together, lifting one at a time. "Your partner?" She pushed her glasses up. "You mean every day?"

Every day?

Laurel hesitated. Oh well, Mrs. Turk would probably make her do it every day anyway. So she answered, "Why not?"

For the first time, she saw Roberta smile a real smile. Laurel noticed again how perfect and how white her teeth were.

"How do you get your teeth so white?" Laurel asked.

Wow, pretty stupid-sounding. *Duh.* But Roberta gave Laurel an earnest look, a look that was serious and warm at the same time.

"You know, it might be because of my skin. My skin's pretty dark, and I think maybe that makes my teeth look whiter."

"You must have gotten a great tan this summer."

"It's not really a tan. I'm like this all the time. I was born with a tan, I guess."

Laurel felt a twinge of embarrassment. "Anyway, I wish my teeth were as nice as yours," she said somewhat lamely. "You're lucky."

"Thanks. I guess I am lucky."

Laurel was used to remarks that elaborately pretended to be modest, remarks like "Oh please, my teeth aren't white at all," or "Your teeth are ten times nicer than mine!" So the simplicity of this comment was almost startling: *I guess I am lucky.* Laurel repeated the words to herself. She would try to use them the next time she received a compliment.

"I wanted to ask you about something," Laurel said, then broke off awkwardly. She did several sit-ups, then continued. "I wanted to talk to you about your... brother, you know, that boy in my class. I keep trying and trying to figure out... He seems to be... well.... There's something strange about him...."

Roberta looked stunned.

It had come out all wrong—insulting! "Wait, that's not what I meant," Laurel said in a rush. "Let me try again."

She began to lay out all the pieces of the puzzle for Roberta. The astonishing computer wizardry. Those striking, impenetrable eyes. The way he seemed to have no feelings. And of course that mystifying remark of his: *In a sense the computer is part of me.*

She remembered another piece and stumbled. She just couldn't tell Roberta about the time she and Jeanie had sneaked into her yard, and Jeanie had spied on her and said that Roberta was peering into a computer as though something were lost inside. Laurel swept that guilty memory aside and finished in a wild burst. "Please tell me, please. What's the thing about computers? What *is* it about computers and your brother?"

Roberta looked down at her knees. "Maybe you should talk to him," she mumbled.

"Get busy over there," called Mrs. Turk. "Let's see those sit-ups."

Roberta began bobbing up and down, up and down, almost violently.

"I can't talk to him myself, I just can't. Please tell me what's going on," Laurel pleaded.

Roberta paused, then touched Laurel's hand very lightly. "You're nice to care," she said in her earnest way. Then her face grew anguished. She did a few more sit-ups—distracted, anguished sit-ups. She lay back on the mat and sighed.

Finally she spoke. "Something strange happened to my brother. After we moved here. But I don't know what exactly."

"Strange? Like what? Was it while he was using a computer?"

When Roberta didn't answer, Laurel burst out: "What do you *think* happened?"

"What do I *think*? Here's what I think. I think that my brother's mind…" She stopped.

"What happened to his mind? It has something to do with computers, right?"

"Maybe so. I mean, yes!" Roberta dropped her voice to a whisper. *"I think his mind… somehow got transferred to the computer."*

"Oh my God… And so is that boy in my class some kind of… computer copy or something?" Was *that* why Roberta had said he wasn't really her brother?

Roberta's lips pressed into a tight line. She pulled away. Her eyes had a miserable look.

Suddenly uneasy, Laurel looked up. Shannon was watching. She was watching Laurel and Roberta from across the gym, and her eyes were hard as marbles.

chapter 11

Shannon's eyes are on Laurel that evening, too. They are watching her from across the room at Felicity Osterman's party. It's Friday night. The party is in an old barn. The only light is from old-fashioned lanterns.

It is chilly in the barn, chilly and dark. Kids standing near the edges are hidden by tall, stretching shadows. Shannon is leaning against one of the barn walls, mostly in shadow. Laurel tells herself to go over and say hello, but decides to stay awhile in the warmer center.

Felicity pushes her way into the middle of the crowd, greeting friends and laughing. Laurel hasn't seen her much this school year.

"Well, hi there, Shady Lady!" Felicity is grinning and wrapping her arms around Laurel. Laurel loves Felicity.

"I hardly ever see you this year!" Felicity exclaims. "It stinks you don't take gymnastics anymore!" Then a long shadow stretches over Felicity and seems to pull her away.

Square dancing has begun. The kids are swinging in and out of darkness. A fiddle wails in the background. *What a strange, strange sound,* Laurel thinks.

Chrissie's face, grinning, looking somehow disembodied, floats in front of Laurel. "We're giving you a ride home, right, Laurel?"

Before Laurel can answer, a tall, thin boy grabs her by the waist. David Holyfield! Her heart speeds up. It can't be! Her heart is pounding.

It is not David Holyfield. This is a boy Laurel has never seen before. He swings her energetically. Then his grip breaks. Laurel stumbles forward and finds herself looking into Collin Forest's snickering face. He locks his arm through hers and begins a series of wild twirls.

Laurel's skull begins to feel squeezed. "Stop," she pants. "I want to take a break." She pulls herself out of the dancing circle and over to the side. Standing against the dark barn wall, she wraps her arms around herself and watches the dancers. Why does this party feel like a movie Laurel is watching?

"I wasn't sure you'd make it," Shannon's voice says right next to her.

Laurel jumps a little. It is a guilty, jittery jump. Things have been so awkward lately with Shannon. She is smiling at Laurel right now, but there is something cold in that smile. It is a hanging-back kind of smile.

Shannon seems to know the girl on her other side, a dark-haired girl Laurel has never seen before. The girl's wavy black hair makes Shannon's look even blonder and silkier than usual.

"This is Justine," Shannon says. "I met her on the Vineyard. She's staying at my house tonight, so Felicity said it was okay to bring her."

Justine has sleepy eyes. They can't be more than halfway open. Her lids are so heavy that her eyes look like they are wearing small hoods.

"Justine just joined my club," Shannon says.

What club? Laurel wonders. *The Cool Club? No, that's impossible.*

A few years earlier Shannon had invented the Cool Club. Laurel was the second member. They used to hold meetings in Shannon's basement. As Laurel remembers it, the only thing they ever did at the meetings was talk about who else should be allowed into the Cool Club. They were little kids then, of course. It seems pretty silly now.

Then Laurel realizes that right now, when Shannon says "my club," she is talking about the Soundview Country Club. Usually Shannon calls it her parents' club. That's what she used to call it, anyway.

Now Shannon is staring down, staring hard. She seems to be staring at Laurel's shoes.

Laurel tries to think of something to say. "Is Aubrey Madison here?" she asks Shannon. "Someone said she was coming."

"Laurel. Please. Aubrey already came and went. She's *gone*. She was here for like five seconds. I mean why should she stay at some stupid barn and freeze her butt off after what's happened to her?"

"Why? What happened to Aubrey?"

"Don't you know?" Shannon responds in a high-pitched voice. She widens her eyes and pauses. "She got a modeling contract! Can you imagine being our age and already having a modeling career? How cool would that be?"

"Wow. Well, I guess if anyone should have a modeling contract, it's Aubrey," Laurel says.

Silence. Shannon and Justine exchange looks.

Why are you looking at each other like that? Laurel wants to ask. But she feels strangely timid. Justine tilts her chin up ever so slightly and gazes at Laurel. It is an idle-looking gaze. She can't seem to be bothered to open her eyes wider.

And Shannon, once again, seems to be staring at Laurel's shoes.

The barn is very chilly. The cold blows through and flickers the lanterns and wiggles the shadows.

"Musical chairs!" a man's voice bellows. When a groan arises, the bellowing voice responds, "Come on, kids, get with it! Back in the nineteenth century, *everyone* played musical chairs—except for babies!"

A row of tall, spindly wooden chairs appears in the center of the barn floor. Each chair faces the opposite way from the chairs on either side of it.

"Hold on a second!" Felicity calls out. She does a series of cartwheels in front of the row of chairs, precise as a knife through the air. Everyone applauds.

Scrape-wail, scrape-wail. The fiddle sounds out of the blackness.

Laurel is caught in a wild chain of dancers circling the row of chairs, waving their limbs to the *scrape-wail* sound.

The fiddle stops. There is a thrashing toward the chairs. Someone pushes Laurel toward a chair and she lands in it sideways, on her hip.

Several chairs are removed. *Scrape-wail.* Laurel shudders as the fiddle starts up again. The chain of dancers reassembles. But now there is less wild thrashing, more tension. Everyone is riveted on the remaining chairs.

The fiddle stops, and the dancers stampede toward the chairs. Some kids land on the floor. Panic rises in Laurel. Why wasn't she focusing more? She heads toward a chair, but no, someone has it. She hurries toward another. It fills before she gets there. Over on the other side, there is still an empty space. Laurel speeds over and flops down in the chair. Her heart is racing. Now she remembers, she hates musical chairs, always hated it.

"Chill out," says a voice to one side. Laurel looks up into Justine's hooded eyes. Justine is spread out lazily one chair away. "It's just a game," she says to Laurel.

When the fiddle music begins again, Laurel tells herself to concentrate. Always have a chair in reach, always have a chair in mind. No more wandering along in a dream. Keep focused.

And so when the music stops, she moves swiftly to the black-runged chair she has targeted. But her legs collapse and she falls. Someone has tripped her.

The last thing Laurel sees before she hits the floor is Justine. Justine is sitting in the black-runged chair. Her eyes are still hooded, but they are laughing, too.

This party isn't fun, thinks Laurel. *No, this is not fun.*

By the time Laurel was dropped off at home, her whole family seemed to be sleeping. She crept up the stairs and into bed, feeling cold.

As she lay in bed, the room seemed to swirl as if she were still dancing. When she closed her eyes, the gauntlet of chairs appeared and the strange wail of the fiddle floated back. Dark and mocking things circled her: the spindly chairs, the shadows, Justine's hooded eyes. Laurel had to sit up to make it all go away.

When she lay back again and closed her eyes, she was in the old climbing tree. Her fingers gripped the thick, corky bark. She was pulling herself from one gnarled branch to the next. She was moving quickly, light as a feather, trying to reach the boy who climbed above her.

He turned around and looked at her. It was David Holyfield. He fixed her with those eyes of his—so pale, so strange somehow. At last Laurel pulled up onto his branch. She moved next to him and looked closer. But she wasn't really looking into his eyes. She was looking into a computer screen that displayed his face. As she reached toward it, the image broke into horizontal stripes and then solid blue. ABORT, RETRY, said the bottom of the screen.

Laurel sat up abruptly. She jumped out of bed and shook herself all over. Maybe she could shake off these weird pictures.

She headed down to the kitchen for a glass of milk. The milk seemed to wake up her appetite, and she got out some crackers and peanut butter. She sat at the kitchen island eating her snack, her mind roaming.

How could a boy's mind get transferred to a computer?

How could a computer make a copy of a boy?

It was ridiculous. It was impossible. It was easier to believe that Nightshade walked through walls right onto Jeanie's bed. That's what Jeanie was now claiming.

Laurel's eyes came to rest just then on a pile of pans leaning against the dish rack. Cookie sheets—what had her mother been baking?

Wait a minute. Cookie sheets. Peanut butter. This might be the way to crack the Nightshade case!

Laurel began to set her trap in silence. First she edged the cookie sheets away from the dish rack, trying not to disrupt the other pans. She laid them flat, side by side, on the kitchen island.

Then she dipped her hand into the peanut butter jar and scooped up as much as she could. Carefully spreading and scooping, she covered both of the cookie sheets with a smooth layer of peanut butter.

Laurel crept to the sink and washed her hands. She tried to keep the water from making splashing noises in the sink.

She found Nightshade on the sofa in the family room and lifted him off. She plopped him down in her parents' room and silently closed the door. Then she tiptoed back to the kitchen for one of the cookie sheets and placed it on the floor right in front of her parents' closed bedroom door.

Carefully balancing the second cookie sheet in front of her, she padded soundlessly upstairs. At the door to her room, she turned and placed the cookie sheet on the floor in the hall, directly in front of the bedroom door. Then she stepped inside her bedroom and shut the door tight.

She looked at Jeanie, sound asleep, wearing faded yellow pajamas. And what a stroke of luck! Those were the pajamas with the feet attached.

Looking down at her own nightshirt, Laurel saw that it now had a peanut butter stripe across the stomach. She quickly changed and slid into bed. This time she fell asleep immediately.

In the morning there was Nightshade on Jeanie's bed as usual. Although the room was filled with sunlight, Jeanie was still sound asleep.

Laurel bolted to the door and looked at the peanut butter–covered cookie sheet just outside. The surface was smooth and perfect. It had not been disturbed.

How on earth had Nightshade gotten into the room?

Laurel tore over to Jeanie's bed and pulled the covers down. Jeanie was sleeping in the same old yellow pajamas that she'd had on in the night. Laurel inspected Jeanie's feet. They were clean.

That kitten *could not have gotten into the room*—it was impossible. Yet here he was, and without a trace of peanut butter, either on his fur or on Jeanie.

Jeanie had begun to stir. But almost as soon as her eyes opened, she clapped her hands behind her head, stretched out on her back, and squinched her eyes shut again. She claimed she wanted to watch a Saturday-morning cartoon called *Needlehead,* about a boy who was half-human, half-porcupine.

Suddenly Dr. Shade's voice boomed out, oddly harsh. "What the *hell* is this? *Who the hell left this pan of peanut butter on the floor?*"

Laurel's stomach did a dive.

Jeanie opened her eyes and looked over. "That's so strange," Jeanie said. "That is really, really strange." She wasn't smiling but her eyes glowed. "He knows we don't say 'hell' in this family."

chapter 12

Nightshade, the kitten that walks through walls. How can it be true?

Is it really true? Jeanie is not to be trusted, of course. But peanut butter doesn't lie. And Laurel's mom is swearing that the parents' bedroom door didn't open—at least not until the unlucky Dr. Shade got up.

And if a kitten can walk through walls, maybe a boy's mind really could disappear into a computer. Somehow these two strange events seem to fit together. Does the one help to explain the other?

"What's the answer, Nightshade?" Laurel murmurs as Nightshade, casually strolling past, makes a last-minute turn to scrape against her legs. Laurel squats down and strokes his jaw. Then she whispers into his ear. "Please tell me, Nightshade, please. What's your secret?"

Nightshade twitches his ears and pulls away. Laurel sighs. "Never mind, you little betrayer."

But Laurel couldn't get these mysteries out of her mind.

"Mom, do you think a computer could make a real boy? Or, like, an almost-real boy?"

"I always find conversations about what's real and what isn't to be pretty rough going. Who am I to say?"

"Well, what do you think?" persisted Laurel. "Is it possible?"

"Possible? Anything is possible. You know, it's even possible that you and I are creations of a computer. Maybe the entire population of the United States was computer-generated and we just don't realize it. Maybe the computer that created us installed a false life-memory in each of us."

Mrs. Shade could be infuriating sometimes. She was just too busy being clever to give a straight answer.

Jeanie, on the other hand, had very definite opinions. "Of course a computer can make a copy of a boy. Computers made hundreds of different kinds of dinosaurs in that movie *Jurassic Park*. Making just one regular boy should be a piece of cake!"

Laurel was not convinced. This wasn't a movie, after all. At least she didn't think so.

She felt glum and adrift somehow. Normally she would have turned to her father, but right now did not seem like the best time. He was probably still working the peanut butter out from under his toenails. So Laurel wandered into the backyard after her mother.

Mrs. Shade was starting some gardening project. "I got these azaleas for six dollars each," she told Laurel triumphantly. "Want to help me plant them?"

"Sure," Laurel answered. Planting flowers sounded soothing.

Her mother handed her a trowel. "Dig a hole about twice the size of the plant's pot," she directed. "The one thing about buying azaleas this time of year, since the flowers are gone, you can't be sure what color they'll be. But for six dollars each, I'm willing to gamble a little."

Laurel began digging. A few minutes later she clanged against rock. Her palm burned where she gripped the trowel. She had not picked a good digging place, she decided. She began a fresh hole about a foot to the left of where she'd started. That spot turned out to have a fat root spreading below the ground. She started digging again at a third location.

"Laurel, are you building your own little mole city?" her mother said sharply. "I thought you wanted to *help* me."

Her voice was so harsh that Laurel just looked down, feeling stung. She stared at her hands. They were remarkably dirty. Each fingernail looked like a sliver from some black moon.

She studied her wrists. She could picture the wrists of the Holyfield boy right now in her mind. Her own wrists seemed almost puffy compared to his.

She could picture his nose, too, in profile. The arch of it was strangely perfect.

Mrs. Shade had hunched down next to Laurel. "I'm sorry I snapped," she said. "To tell you the truth, sometimes gardening gets me a little crabby." She reached over and brushed Laurel's hair back from her face.

"Did you know that azaleas are practically your cousins?" Laurel's mother was smiling. "I think azaleas are related to mountain laurel. You know that's how you got your name, don't you?"

At Laurel's look of surprise, she continued. "Daddy and I used to go backpacking a lot before you were born, and we'd see lots of mountain laurel on the trail. We really loved it. It was sort of one of those romantic things couples like to share. So when we found out we were going to have a little girl, we wanted to name you Laurel."

"Why didn't you ever tell me that before?" Laurel asked. "That's really cool!"

What an exciting new possession this was—a name with a real reason behind it. A romantic reason! Laurel felt a new appreciation for her name.

She sat back on her heels. Once again the Holyfield boy's profile floated in front of her. What computer could design such an oddly perfect nose? She traced its curve in the air before her.

"You seem a little distracted," her mother said carefully. "And you know, that business with the peanut butter... well, you just don't seem like yourself. Is something bothering you?"

"I don't know," Laurel said.

"You don't know. I see."

"What I mean is, I *am* distracted, but I don't exactly know why. My mind keeps going back to the same things. The same weird things."

"Is one of those weird things a boy?" her mother asked gently.

Was he a boy? That was one of the big questions.

"I don't know," Laurel said again. Then she had to laugh at how indecisive she sounded. "I'm sorry. I guess I mean yes," she said, feeling sheepish. "I guess one of the weird things is a boy."

"A special boy—a boy that you like?"

Laurel put her hand over her eyes. Why wasn't this simple?

"I don't *know*," she said for the third time, this time in a high-pitched, helpless voice. "If you can believe that. I don't even know if I like him. I don't see how I could. But for some reason I keep thinking about him. Isn't this weird?"

"It doesn't sound that weird to me," said Mrs. Shade. "What it sounds like is like maybe you have your first real crush."

Wouldn't that be something. Her first real crush, and it wasn't even on a real boy! "Oh, Mom. I don't think you'd say that if you knew him. He's not... he's not like a regular kid."

"Well, this is kind of intriguing," her mother said. "Could this have anything to do with the computer-generated boy you were wondering about earlier?"

Oh *man*. It sounded so ridiculous. How much longer could her mother keep a straight face?

Laurel groped for words. "The thing is, this kid is... I don't know. Strange. The other guys call him an android." She waited to receive some clever motherly barb.

"Detached," her mother suggested, with unexpected gentleness. "Like he doesn't have feelings."

"Y-e-e-sss." Laurel didn't like the way it sounded. "But he—I think maybe he needs some kind of help. But there probably isn't anything I can do."

Mrs. Shade looked thoughtful. Then she began brushing the dirt off the knees of her pants with vigor but no real success. She was still looking down at her knees when she spoke again.

"There's always one thing you can do. You can always ask."

Something tugged Laurel toward the trail, to the place where the climbing tree had been. The spot still had a little magic. A warm-earth smell filled her nose. Tarzan vines squiggled down against a dark, leafy background. The air carried a high, sweet tinkling sound. What *was* that sound? Was it real?

It was a real sound, not Laurel's imagination. It was from some amazing wind chime. Such delicate patterns of sound!

No, it couldn't be a wind chime. The patterns were too perfect for a wind chime.

The sweet sound drew Laurel forward. She walked to the edge of the yard of the little white-shingled house. The Holyfields' house.

Laurel's feet moved across the lawn. The sound was stronger now. She tiptoed toward the front door, hardly breathing. Her heart thumped. She stood on the top step.

She could see Roberta through a window, playing the piano. Her head and shoulders hunched forward in a passionate arch. Her dark ponytail hugged her back.

Laurel shouldn't just stand there; she should ring the doorbell. She should either ring the doorbell or leave. Laurel turned and took a step down.

Oh, go ahead, ring the bell. What's the big deal? She pivoted and again stepped up to the front door.

Wait a minute, not today. She was still a little grubby from gardening. Another day would make more sense.

Everything was suddenly still. The piano music had stopped! Panic grabbed Laurel.

Roberta was waving at her through the window.

Inside, the house was crammed. Its rooms seemed unusually small, and they were filled to capacity—with furniture, music CDs, books, more CDs. Every available inch of wall had been used to display some sort of artwork.

In the front room, opposite the piano, an extremely long table ran against the wall. The table was covered with computer equipment. Keyboards, mouse pads, printers. Not one monitor, but several. Other unidentifiable metal boxes, sprouting electrical cords. Black diskettes, scattered around like sections of the Sunday paper.

Laurel let out a gasp. "How many computers do you *have*?" she asked in wonder.

"Hmm. Maybe six," Roberta answered. "Not counting the laptops."

Laurel's eyebrows shot up. Then she looked back toward the piano. "Please play some more," she urged.

Roberta complied. The notes began floating, building, filling the room.

Laurel had never heard anything so bewitching. She sat in a small wooden chair on one side of the piano, where she could watch Roberta's face while she played.

The reflection of piano keys filled Roberta's glasses, concealing her eyes. Her large white teeth gently bit into her lower lip. She was in her own little heaven.

Laurel closed her eyes. The musical notes seemed to lift her chair toward the ceiling. "What are you playing?" she whispered, not wanting to break the spell.

"Chopin. One of his waltzes. He's my favorite. I play Chopin and I feel like, I don't know, like I'm building something. And it's, like, solid, but it's delicate, too, and just so totally *perfect*."

These were not the sort of feelings Laurel herself had ever had. But the music was getting inside her. It was buoying her. Now it was drawing designs in front of her. She tried describing the designs to Roberta, who glowed.

"Hey, let's try something. I'll pick a painting in this room and try to play music about it. Then let's see if you can guess which one I'm doing."

Roberta bent her head down and began playing again. The sweet tinkling made Laurel think of springtime. It sounded like birds, maybe like raindrops. Wait a minute. The painting hanging right above the piano. A tree whose leaves were being touched by sunlight; why, the music seemed to be describing it. "Aha!" Laurel pointed.

Roberta stopped playing and applauded. "You're good at this." After a pause she added softly but with twinkling eyes, "Or could this be beginner's luck?"

Laurel laughed. "No way!" So they did another painting, and another, and another. A blurry circus scene. A mother holding a baby. Brightly colored, fantastic animal shapes. More than half the time, Laurel guessed the picture Roberta had in mind.

The insides of Laurel's ears were tingling, probably because they'd never worked so hard before. It was exciting. And to be able to make music like Roberta—that would be miraculous. Before she realized it, Laurel let out a loud sigh.

Roberta pushed her glasses down her nose and peered over them questioningly. "Holy smoke," she said. "That sure didn't sound happy."

Holy smoke, Laurel repeated to herself. *Now, there's an odd expression.* It was straight from an old black-and-white movie. Something her great-uncle Walter might say.

Out loud she said to Roberta, "I'm just thinking how cool it must be to be able to play the piano. Do you think it's too late for me to start lessons?"

"No. No, definitely not. But I wouldn't wait too much longer. In fact, you should probably start in the next ten minutes or so."

The comical sternness of Roberta's arched brows made Laurel smile. But Roberta was already squirming off the piano bench. "Come on! I've got some of my old piano books upstairs, if you want to look at them."

For some time—how long?—Laurel had been totally absorbed in the music game. But now, as they headed for the stairs, a rushing feeling started up inside her. *He* was around here someplace. "I hope we aren't bothering anyone," she whispered. The rushing feeling was getting stronger.

"It's okay. My dad's not here right now." Roberta's feet were flashing up the stairs ahead of Laurel.

Laurel pushed words out of her mouth one at a time. "What about your... your... well, your mom?"

"It's just the three of us." Roberta didn't turn around.

Just the three of them—yikes. No mother. Were the parents divorced? Had the mother died? But Roberta didn't volunteer any more information, and Laurel had already asked too much.

But where was David? Where *was* he?

Roberta's room was tiny, and every bit as crammed as the downstairs. A large desk had somehow been squeezed into it, along with a narrow bed, a CD player, and an overflowing bookcase. The only place to sit was on the bed.

Above the bed hung an oval-framed sketch of a man with a long nose and longish hair. "Who's that?" Laurel asked.

"That's Chopin."

"Is he your hero or something?"

"I guess so."

Who would my hero be? Laurel wondered silently. No one came to mind.

Roberta seemed to take the silence as a request for explanation. "Chopin was *so cool*. It's like he poured his whole self into making something for the world. Something so beautiful. And then he died while he was still in his thirties."

Something in Laurel's chest went *ping*. It had nothing to do with Chopin. It was Roberta. She cared so much. In the glow of Roberta's pure passion for this musician, Laurel's own concerns seemed childish and shabby. She closed her eyes and desperately wished to care about something the way Roberta cared about music.

The back of Laurel's neck prickled. With a quick jerk, she looked toward the door. Roberta's brother was looking at her. His face was blank as a stone.

Then he turned and left.

chapter 13

A ll Laurel wants to do is bolt.
    She'd felt so exhilarated when Roberta first made the
suggestion: "Look, why not just ask my brother some questions?" Roberta had said. "That's one way to get to the bottom
of what's going on in his head—don't you think?"

But now that they are actually here, standing next to him
at one of the computers, Laurel just wants to run madly from
the room. Her thoughts about minds and computers have
become vague, bizarre, impossible to put into words. And she
is paralyzed by a flustered sensation she's never felt before. The
earlier rushing feeling is now a roar in her head.

When she finally managed to choke out a question, it was broad
and impersonal: *Could information from a brain be transferred to a computer, and replaced with some kind of computer intelligence?* Now the
Holyfield boy was responding.

"A human brain and a computer both operate in basically
binary fashion. That means that, potentially, they are communica-
tions compatible."

Even as he talked, his fingers were moving nonstop on the keyboard, so that his low, precise voice meshed with the keyboard's

rattling sound. He seemed to need constant contact with the computer. "*Binary* means two choices," he continued. "In computers, each bit is an electronic switch that's either open or closed, off or on."

Laurel watched his undulating fingers and looked at the arch of his oddly perfect nose and felt a sort of ache between her lungs. Meanwhile the roar in her head continued.

He, on the other hand, had no feelings at all—judging from his voice, at least. He sounded like a Vulcan on *Star Trek*. "When you analyze it," he said, "you can say anything in computer language as long as you have enough bits."

In spite of her inner turmoil, Laurel remembered the Yankee scoreboard. How the light switching between on and off created words, pictures, motion. And how Mr. Schmitt had told her that computers did the same thing, just much faster and with tremendously more switches. She turned her head slowly, surveying the room. For a fleeting moment the whole world dissolved into intricate layered patterns of off and on.

Meanwhile the boy was saying something astonishing. "There's another key similarity between a computer and a human brain. They both operate by means of electricity. The human brain isn't understood as well as computers, but it definitely uses electrical impulses to transmit information."

Human brains work by electricity? Laurel said to herself. *No way!*

He was saying that the brain had billions of neurons that sent electrical impulses, and that each neuron worked basically like an electrical switch in a computer—on or off, impulse or no impulse. Nothing in between. The electrical impulses could also release chemical packets and cause other subtle interactions. Yet the main reason the brain could do complicated things was because of the huge number of neurons, not because the neurons themselves were complicated. Like computers.

"In theory, then, a human brain and a computer could directly exchange information."

Only after a long strange silence did Laurel realize he had finished. Then he lowered his head a notch or two and turned his back to her. His typing speed increased. She was being dismissed.

It was humiliating. Once again her body started urging her to bolt—just bolt—but she managed to mumble a thanks and walk out with a sliver of dignity. Roberta followed.

At the foot of the stairs Laurel halted and cursed herself. She cursed her spineless, chickenhearted failure to ask him anything meaningful. *Don't be such a wimp*, she lectured herself. *Go back and talk to him, ask him about himself. Just don't look in his eyes—they get you too flustered.*

She headed back. Roberta stayed, one hand on the banister, face confused.

The Holyfield boy looked up from the monitor.

Laurel rammed aside her shyness, began shoveling words out as fast as possible. "What I really want to know about is *you*. I'm trying to figure out if you're... a... a regular kid or not."

The silvery green eyes drove into her. Laurel's face got hot.

After an excruciating silence he answered. "On what basis can *anyone* say with certainty that *anyone* is a 'regular kid'?" Was there a trace of contempt in his voice? "We can say we *think* we are, but that's not really answering the question, is it? What is it exactly that produced our *thinking*?"

He thought she was a fool—she could feel it! Oh *why* had she opened her mouth again? Her face was like a balloon, filling up with shame. *I must get out of this room before I explode from embarrassment,* she thought, and fled for the stairs.

"Man oh man," Laurel burst out when she and Roberta were back upstairs. "What was he saying?"

Roberta took off her glasses. She scrunched her eyebrows together. "Pretty confusing all right." She looked worried.

Laurel's mind was spinning. "That thing about how can we know where our thoughts come from—wow."

She closed her eyes to help herself think. One thing seemed very clear: regular kids just did not, *could not,* have such thoughts. It was so sci-fi, so incredible, but the puzzle pieces did seem to be fitting. *There's a cyborg in your future....*

"You know what I think, Roberta? I just don't think a real boy would answer like that." She paused, gaining conviction. "I don't even think he *could* answer like that. Not even if his life depended on it!"

Roberta looked disheartened. In fact, she looked almost ill. All at once Laurel felt bad for her. She put on a brisk, jolly manner.

"Look, maybe we can fix this. Let's take it a step at a time. So first of all, if that guy isn't really your brother—what do you think we should call him?"

Roberta seemed so lost in thought Laurel began doubting she'd heard. But eventually Roberta did answer: "Computer Dave?" she offered.

Then Roberta made an odd sniffing noise. Her shoulders started shaking. She was breaking down. She was starting to cry. No, wait— she was *laughing,* Laurel realized. It was a quaking, wheezy laugh that Roberta was trying to hold down. But it was coming out, all right, out of her mouth and now Laurel's, too. Funny how a person could feel so confused and worried and so... giddy, all at the same time.

Just then a clock chimed downstairs. Two o'clock! Laurel could hardly believe it. "Yikes! I've got to get home right away—I'm going to get killed!" She flew downstairs. "See ya!"

Roberta called down after her. "When, do you think?"

"Pardon?"

"*When* will I see you, Laurel?"

Laurel hesitated. "Whenever!" she shouted as she opened the

front door. She added an extra dose of gaiety to the word, hoping to cover its vagueness.

Outside, she was suddenly terrified. She would hate to be spotted coming out of the Holyfield house. She needed to get out of this yard and onto the public trail as quickly as possible.

At the spot where the tree had been, something slowed her; then she stopped. She heard piano notes begin to rise and float on the air once more. For a split second, she saw an image of the climbing tree, twisty and spreading and enchanted. And like a sudden breeze, a memory blew past, a memory of that perfectly free feeling up in the climbing tree.

She'd almost forgotten about the tree! This computer stuff was distracting her. And somehow the more she saw of Roberta, the farther removed she seemed from the climbing tree situation.

Why had they cut it down? It was the father, of course. The mysterious software-developer father who was never there. Would it all have been different somehow if a mother had been around? Maybe if Laurel got to know Roberta better, she would be able to ask her. But she would have to find exactly the right moment. There was something almost breakable about Roberta.

Laurel examined the stump. It looked even darker than when she'd first seen it. Why *was* the wood so dark? She remembered the article about Amur cork trees—she kept forgetting to ask her mom about it. That article had said cork trees were supposed to have light wood, not dark.

That same article also said that Amur cork trees came from China. Why would an exotic cork tree from China be growing on a nature trail? Maybe the climbing tree hadn't been an Amur cork tree after all. Maybe it was just a regular Westchester tree. Except that everyone said there had never been another one like it.

A Chestnut Knoll tree, but not a chestnut tree. Laurel wondered vaguely where the chestnut trees were that the town had been named after. Or maybe there was just one really spectacular chestnut tree somewhere. It would be pretty cool to figure out which chestnut tree the town was named after. It had to be on a knoll somewhere, right?

When Laurel banged in through the back door of her house, her mother immediately scowled. "We've been looking all over for you. I called Shannon trying to find you. I think we're going to have to take Jeanie to the emergency room."

A Skittle had gotten stuck up Jeanie's nose and no one could dislodge it.

"It's getting covered with stuff," Jeanie called from the sofa, where she sat red-eyed and cross-legged, surrounded by crumpled wads of tissue. "What's the word, Laurel, what's the polite word?"

Laurel stared at her sister, dumbfounded.

"What's the polite word, Laurel, *what is it?*" Jeanie started screeching. *"You know it! Tell me what that polite word is!"*

Now Jeanie's entire face was bright red. She jerked her body, and a sort of hiccuping-choking sound came out. She shoved a tissue in front of her face and coughed something into it. It was the Skittle, faded to a pale pink. It was covered in a slimy cloud.

"Nasal mucus," Laurel said.

Mrs. Shade moaned. "Thank goodness." She plopped down next to Jeanie, looking drained. Dr. Shade came over and wrapped his arms around Jeanie. "I was beginning to think you'd have to have a Skittle-ectomy," he said, moving his soft beard over the top of Jeanie's head. Even Nightshade appeared and rubbed consolingly against Jeanie's shins. It was remarkable, really, how Jeanie could stick a Skittle up her nose and practically become Joan of Arc.

Dr. Shade smiled over at Laurel. "You didn't get to taste one of my fried-banana and cream cheese sandwiches. I made them for lunch but we couldn't find you."

Laurel decided that this remark did not absolutely require her to explain where she'd been.

"I had to tinker with the original recipe a little," Dr. Shade went on. "The original recipe calls for *peanut butter.*"

Laurel smiled a sheepish smile. At least now he could joke about it.

"Dad, sometime I want to try to find the chestnut tree that Chestnut Knoll is named after. Do you have any idea where it would be? It must be on a hill somewhere, a knoll."

"You know, Laurel, it's a sad thing about American chestnut trees. They don't really exist anymore. They were pretty much wiped out by chestnut blight in the early twentieth century."

"You mean they're extinct? Like dinosaurs?"

"Basically."

Jeanie and Laurel looked at each other in horror. "That's terrible!" they cried in unison.

"Well, yes. Yes, it's terrible, but it happens every so often with trees. Some disease comes along and kills off a whole species. When I was a kid, it was Dutch elm disease. All the elm trees on my street got sick and died. And now, you know, there aren't many elms around either."

But this whole darn town is named after chestnut trees, Laurel protested to herself. For them not to exist anymore seemed outrageous.

Some tracing of David Holyfield was inhabiting Laurel's head, like a ghost she could not drive away. Even when she thought about other things, she was thinking about him, too. And as she lay in bed that night, he totally filled her mind.

Computer Dave, she said to herself. *The one who thinks I'm an imbecile.*

But that wasn't really true. He didn't think she was an imbecile.

He didn't think anything about her at all. He didn't care in the slightest what she thought—what anyone thought. That was what made him so different. He genuinely didn't care what other people thought of him. He didn't care about where he fit in, or whether he fit anywhere at all.

Oh man. So weird. Was her mind caught up in David Holyfield or Computer Dave?

Suddenly she found herself telling Jeanie everything. She had no choice. The words just started stampeding out of her mouth.

She described all about being at the Holyfields'. About the real David versus Computer Dave. His assertions that a brain and a computer could exchange their contents. His nonhuman eyes. His detachment. The software-developer father. She tried to present all the pieces as dispassionately as possible.

But Jeanie was enthralled. "The guy is part computer! It could be! We know computers are always messing things up, right? So why couldn't there be some kind of mix-up of files? Why couldn't it happen? Everything in David's brain gets sent to the computer, and then gets replaced in his brain with some computer file. Makes sense to me. You know, Laurel, this is really important stuff you're working on!"

Jeanie's interest was strangely touching. "A sister is a built-in buddy," Laurel's grandmother liked to say. Maybe she had something there.

Laurel stared up at the bumpy bedroom ceiling. Her time in the Holyfield house had turned into a kind of dream. Had she really spent all that time with him?

Right next to him. Talking. They'd had a conversation. She'd made a complete fool of herself, true. But you had to start somewhere.

Was this what a crush felt like? Whatever it was, it was confusing. Laurel began a poem.

What are you, David Holyfield? Are you really real?
Tell me how to find you. Tell me what I feel.
Could I have a crush on a computer? Has my
      humanoid heart been won?
And do computers ever love? Just answer off or on.

That last line was not the ending, though. This was a poem that could not be finished. How could she finish a poem when she didn't even know if she was writing about a person or a thing?

Laurel woke up much later, in the pitch black, with a trapped feeling. Something was pushing against her. It was Jeanie.

"What do you think you're doing, Jeanie?" Laurel moaned. "What time is it?"

Jeanie just kept pushing her way closer to the center of the bed. She was using her knees to prod Laurel toward the side.

"Go back to your own bed!"

"No," Jeanie said firmly.

"Puh-leeze get out of my bed! What's the matter with you anyway?"

"There is a very scary movie playing in my head right now," Jeanie said. "I think I might be too young to watch it."

You strange little thing, Laurel thought. She turned over and tried to look at Jeanie's face in the darkness. Jeanie's skin looked pure white, and her eyes looked huge and black.

Laurel sighed. "Okay, tell me about the movie."

"It's too scary."

"Okay, then don't tell me," Laurel said, and turned away.

A minute later there was a small tap on her shoulder. "Do movies get less scary if you talk about them?" Jeanie whispered.

"Usually," Laurel said. She reached in Jeanie's direction and, after some fumbling, placed her hand on Jeanie's kneecap.

"All right then, here's the plot," Jeanie said matter-of-factly. "It's nighttime. I am lost in a jungle and it's filled with wild animals. Their teeth are long and sparkly. They're waiting for me. I start using my pocket scanner and my laptop computer to do a search. I do a global search, for *bad animals,* and the computer shows me where they are. But then my computer freezes."

"Wait, this isn't making sense," Laurel said. "What's the part about a scanner?"

"I use the scanner to scan the jungle and then I feed that information into the computer. Then the computer does a search and lights things up on the monitor, sort of like on a map. At least that's what it does until it freezes."

A search! Laurel sat up in bed.

"A global search," she said out loud. The phrase had a nice ring to it. "A global search," she repeated.

"What do you need to search for?" Jeanie asked.

"For David! I wonder if this might be a way to find him."

"Hmmm," Jeanie said. "Maybe so. But you'd probably have to do a separate search for every program in the computer. And what if he fell into a crack between programs or something?"

Laurel thought for a minute. Jeanie was right. Unless there was some way to do a search of everything in the computer at the same time. Anyway, she would head over to the Holyfields' first thing in the morning. "Oh, Jeanie! This might be it—thanks!"

"That's okay," Jeanie said.

"Maybe you could get back in your own bed now."

"First I have to check if that jungle thing is still on," Jeanie said, and shut her eyes. "No, it's okay now. I think now it's *National Geographic.*" And she slid off the bed and into the darkness.

A moment later, Laurel called softly, as something of an afterthought: "Jeanie, is Nightshade in your bed?"

"Not yet," Jeanie whispered back.

chapter 14

Anticipation—that's what Laurel is feeling when she wakes up the next morning, but she doesn't quite know why.

Then a picture of David Holyfield is there in front of her. The global search! The thought is somehow thrilling.

She begins planning in earnest. She obviously needs to search the computer in the Holyfield house. But where can she tell her parents she is going?

"Good *night*." Jeanie is greeting Laurel, mouth serious but eyes sparkling.

"It's eight o'clock in the morning, Jeanie. You are so cuckoo."

"It's Opposite Day," Jeanie says meaningfully.

Laurel groans. She hates Opposite Day. From now until the end of the day Jeanie will respond only to inversions. You're supposed to say the opposite of what you really mean. What's more, the inversions have to be done in a very particular way, and Jeanie is the sole judge of their correctness.

Just now, for example, Mrs. Shade asks them to get dressed, and Jeanie informs her that it is Opposite Day. When Mrs. Shade says, "Then don't get dressed," Jeanie shouts gleefully, "Get UNdressed, you mean!"

Mrs. Shade shows clenched teeth. "I hate Opposite Day."
"No you don't," Jeanie calls after her. "You LOVE it!"

When Laurel reached the bottom of the stairs, Dr. Shade handed her the phone. She was surprised to hear Shannon's voice on the other end.

Shannon wanted to know about Laurel's disappearance the day before. "Your mother was so totally like having a fit. She was like, 'I've tried everywhere.' So where *did* you go? I had *no idea.*" Shannon paused, then repeated the last words with a dramatic roll. "I had absolutely *no idea.* I thought maybe you were at someone's house or something, but I couldn't think of whose."

A strange wild guilt roared through Laurel. She didn't know how to answer. "You know how mothers can be," she offered weakly.

"I know how *your* mother can be," Shannon said. "But anyway, I couldn't figure out whose house you could possibly be at."

Laurel began to stammer. "So… did you… were you thinking about getting together today?"

"I can't, not on Sunday," Shannon said. "Have to hang with the family."

"Oh, okay. I guess I'll see you tomorrow at school."

"If you go to school tomorrow, that's your business, but you're not going to see *me* there."

"Why not?"

"Because, *duh,* it's a three-day weekend, remember? *Duh?*" Shannon giggled.

Laurel felt foolish. She'd forgotten that tomorrow the school would be closed for Rosh Hashanah, the Jewish New Year.

Now Shannon's voice softened. "Seriously, Laurel. Can I tell you something? I was really worried. It was scary. I'm just glad everything's okay. I was afraid something happened to you."

That was nice of her, Laurel thought as she hung up.

Nevertheless, she was slightly relieved she would not be seeing Shannon.

But the Holyfield house had lost all appeal. Totally. Now the thought of going there brought back the same wild, guilty, nervous feeling that Shannon's voice had triggered.

It would not be a good idea to have Shannon thinking that Laurel and Roberta were friends, people who got together every day. It wouldn't be fair to Roberta to have her thinking that way either. And this friendship… it wasn't a friendship, but whatever it was, it was better to keep it secret. How could Laurel explain it to the kids at school?

And as for the global search idea, well, in the morning light the whole thing seemed pretty laughable. How could a human brain possibly disappear into a computer? It was ridiculous. Wasn't it?

The sad fact was she just didn't know enough. She needed to do some research. "I'm going to the library as soon as it opens," Laurel announced.

Mrs. Shade looked up from the newspaper. "Fine. I think it opens at noon today. Why don't you take Jeanie?"

"I'd rather go by myself."

Dr. Shade frowned. "Come on, Laurel, take your sister. Jeanie, finish your breakfast."

"It's Opposite Day, Dad!" Jeanie trumpeted.

"Then don't finish your breakfast."

"You mean START your breakfast!"

"I hate Opposite Day," Dr. Shade muttered with a look so disgusted Jeanie did not push further.

Laurel decided to make one more attempt. "Well, I guess I'll be leaving for the library now. See you later, everyone."

Dr. Shade turned the disgusted look on Laurel. He spoke in a firm, flat voice. "Not without your sister."

So Laurel and Jeanie set off on bicycles for the Chestnut Knoll library.

Jeanie still saw no reason to take the training wheels off her bike. She pedaled regally, slowly, helmeted head held high. She also refused to wear a backpack. Instead, she insisted on putting the return books in her bike basket, where they kept bouncing out. When Jeanie wasn't stopping to pick them up, she was drifting down the street, the training wheels giving her bike the appearance of a slow-motion chariot.

At the library Laurel struggled to stretch her chain around both bikes. Jeanie's training wheels made it hard to get them close enough. "When are you going to stop being a baby and take off these stupid training wheels?" Laurel grumbled.

Jeanie was not offended. "Know what I'm going to do? I'm going to look for books about wild animals. I think I should confront my fears. So what kind of books are you going to get, Laurel?"

I'm going to learn everything I can about computers, Laurel thought. *If the real David Holyfield really is lost inside a computer, I'm going to find him. Either that or I'll satisfy myself that this is all as ridiculous as it sounds.*

But she was not in the mood to share these thoughts with Jeanie. Instead, after a pause, she answered: "Maybe a book about writing poetry. It's so hard to write a poem."

"No it isn't," Jeanie declared. "At least not in Turbish. *Everything* rhymes in Turbish."

Laurel finally clicked the bike lock shut and straightened up. She looked out over the park next to the library, its green expanse crisscrossed by narrow concrete pathways. Even though the day was somewhat overcast, the park was peppered with Frisbee throwers, leaping dogs, and skateboarders.

Two girls were sitting on a bench at the edge of the park, right near the bike rack. They were swinging their legs in time. One was blond, one dark. They looked up and stared at Laurel.

It was Shannon and Justine.

"Now, there's a Shady character," Shannon said coolly, repeating a nickname the boys sometimes used for Laurel.

As Laurel stepped toward them, she forced her mouth into a smile, but it was as hard as doing a push-up.

"Here with your sister," Shannon commented.

And I thought you had to hang with the family, Laurel thought. But she just did another one of the push-up smiles.

Justine looked bored.

Laurel searched for something to talk about. "So where do you go to school, Justine?"

"Private school," Justine answered languidly.

"Pause the conversation!" Jeanie cried shrilly.

Laurel ignored her. "Is your school someplace in Westchester?"

"Uh-huh," Justine said in an uninterested voice.

"Justine's dad is on the Town Conservation Board," Shannon suddenly remarked. She looked at Justine. "Guess they must be pretty busy, getting ready for that meeting about the climbing tree, huh?"

Justine shrugged.

Shannon then turned toward Laurel. "So what do the Holyfields have to say about this whole thing?"

"I don't know." Laurel's voice rose in spite of her. "I mean, why would I know?"

"Just thought you might," Shannon said.

"Pause the conversation!" Jeanie repeated, this time even more insistently than before.

From under their hoods, Justine's eyes stared out at Jeanie for several seconds. Slowly, her gaze rotated toward Laurel. "Does your sister think we're in a video or something?"

Laurel chuckled. "It's like everything's a video to Jeanie."

Shannon and Justine stared back, unsmiling.

"See you guys later," Laurel said weakly. She headed toward the library steps, Jeanie tugging stubbornly at her arm.

Once inside the library door Laurel whirled toward Jeanie. "Stop bothering me! Stop pulling my arm like that!"

Abruptly, Jeanie stopped walking. She looked up at Laurel with troubled eyes.

"I need some help, Laurel, please. Please help me."

Please! Well, well, well. A "please" from Jeanie was so unusual that now Laurel was the one stopping in her tracks. She searched Jeanie's face.

Jeanie's lip seemed to be wobbling. Her eyes looked even more enormous than usual.

Laurel was baffled. "What's wrong?" she asked. Then she detected a bathroom smell, a bad bathroom smell. "Oh no. Jeanie. You didn't. Tell me you didn't." Laurel was horrified.

Jeanie shut her eyes, and her lip wobbled more noticeably.

"What do you expect me to do?" Laurel moaned.

Jeanie stood motionless, her eyes shut.

"You're in second grade now! How could you do something so gross?"

Jeanie's eyes were still shut. "I tried to pause the conversation and no one would listen," she whispered. "And if I just tore out of there, those girls probably would have said something really mean to you."

A peculiar feeling flooded into Laurel's heart, a tender, achy feeling.

She reached for Jeanie's hand. Jeanie's fingers immediately curled around her own. They felt thin but soft, a little like dried apricots. Together they walked, ever so slowly, to the bathroom.

Laurel helped Jeanie into one of the stalls. She went out to the sink and brought back a wad of damp paper towels. Inside the stall, as she handed the towels to Jeanie one by one, a wispy memory floated past, something about a long-ago birthday party and being too polite to excuse herself and ending up in the same mess Jeanie was in now.

"This really ain't that bad, kid," she said to Jeanie. "Now just lose the underpants"—pointing with one foot at a metal receptacle near the toilet—"and we're in good shape."

The outer bathroom door banged open. Peals of laughter began bouncing off the bathroom walls. "Quick, put your legs up," Laurel whispered. "Don't let people see we're in here together."

The kids who had just come into the bathroom were chattering noisily. "No way," one of them was saying. "It's not like this is... the *inner city* or something."

This comment drew squeals from a second voice. "Swear to God!"

Laurel instantly recognized the second voice. It was Shannon's.

Shannon continued. "It's true. *They actually sleep in the same bedroom.*"

More giggles. Then Shannon's voice again. "Isn't that little sister a total freak? Isn't she just too weird for words? The parents are really weird, too. You should see them together. The mother is like a mile taller than the dad. I'm serious. They're just, I mean, weird. And could you believe those shoes Laurel was wearing at Felicity's party? It's like she's getting as weird as her sister. And acting so buddy-buddy with the tree killers. I mean it, I never realized what a weirdo she is. No wonder no one likes her anymore."

The feeling in Laurel's stomach was like a fast ride down in an elevator. When the elevator stopped at the bottom, she was in a dream. She could hear voices outside the bathroom stall, but they were from some other unreal place.

Until this moment Laurel had never really questioned that she was liked. She had never really questioned that Shannon was her friend. Now the world had flipped inside out. And she, Laurel, was a weirdo.

Laurel's eyes stuck on a spot in front of her, wide open but not seeing anything. Her eyes stayed stuck that way long after Shannon and Justine had left. *No wonder no one likes her anymore.*

I will never leave this stall, Laurel thought numbly. *And I will never be happy again.*

When her eyes finally regained their focus, she saw Jeanie's face tilted up at her. Jeanie's eyes were glistening in a way that Laurel had never seen.

Jeanie reached over, and her dried-apricot fingers interwove themselves with Laurel's. "It's okay, Laurel," she whispered.

The glistening in Jeanie's eyes had condensed into a single tear, which now made its way silently down her cheek. Unexpectedly, she rubbed her head into Laurel's stomach. "It's okay, Laurel. *Weirdo* means something really good in Turbish."

Laurel looked up from her reading and glanced out the library window. The world was so clear! When did the day get so beautiful? The edges of the autumn leaves had a new sharpness, and the clouds blazed white against the sky. It was as if the whole world had had a cleaning. All the dirt and junk had been washed away, leaving only pure, solid things.

She was thrilled by what she was reading. At first, and for some time after the bathroom incident, Laurel hadn't been able to read a word. She had simply sat at the library table, mind roaring, pages swimming. But her concentration now was incredible. She was racing through the stacks of books in front of her, books about electricity, computer science, the human brain, artificial intelligence. The books were piled so high that Laurel had to stretch her neck to see Jeanie sitting across from her. Jeanie was lost in a book called *Apes Are People, Too!*

Laurel had begun her research skeptically. But everything she read confirmed what Computer Dave had said. There were crucial similarities between the human brain and computers.

All the books pointed out common elements between computers and brains. Most of the authors went on to emphasize that a human brain was vastly more complex than any computer—with its chemical processes, and its billions upon billions of circuits formed by the linking of neurons—and concluded that computers could never become as sophisticated as the human brain. But one book, a new book with a bright blue cover, insisted that computers would surpass the capabilities of the human mind within a few decades.

Why hadn't she known this before? Why didn't people talk about this all the time? Laurel couldn't get enough. To think that brains were just flesh-and-blood computers! The ultimate computer, someone had said.

Laurel kept getting stuck on one issue, though. No present-day computer had anywhere near enough capacity to store all the information contained in a human brain. A brain had as many as a hundred billion neurons, and each neuron might have a thousand separate connections between itself and its neighbors. That added up to something like a hundred trillion connections. So it seemed impossible that a boy's mind could be contained in a computer, at least for the present.

"This is so cool, Laurel!" Jeanie was whispering. "It says here that ninety-eight percent of *our* DNA is exactly the same as DNA for *chimpanzees*!"

Laurel gaped at her sister. Then, the lightning bolt: *it wouldn't have to be the whole thing.*

It wouldn't have to be the whole mind! Laurel grabbed Jeanie's book and started reading.

Jeanie was right. According to the book, only two percent of human DNA differed from chimp DNA. And only *one-quarter of a percent* of human DNA varied from person to person. The other 99.75 percent was identical in *all* human beings! Just a *quarter of one percent* was all that made a person an individual.

Maybe the same thing was true for neurons! She turned back to her own books. Sure enough—now it jumped off the page at her—most of a brain's neurons were needed just to keep its own life processes going and to operate the body's basic machinery. Only a small fraction was particular to an individual.

To store a quarter of a percent of a person's genetic or neural information in a computer was not too far-fetched. In fact, the author claimed that all the code necessary to define an individual could be contained on a floppy disk!

It *was* possible, then, entirely possible, that only the essential part of David—his Davidness—had been transferred to a computer. It would explain how Computer Dave could continue to look and function basically normally. It also explained how a present-day computer could have enough capacity to contain the real David.

There was still one puzzle. In order to exchange files, to get stored in a computer, you'd have to be *directly* linked to it. David Holyfield himself, not the keyboard but David's own brain, had to have been communicating directly with the computer. Was *that* possible?

The library would be closing soon, Laurel realized. She rushed back one last time to the computer section and bumped hard, nose-first, into the elbow of a man in a black T-shirt. Water filled her eyes and her nose began throbbing. She stepped back.

It was Mr. Schmitt, the computer teacher. In the casual black T-shirt, he was almost unrecognizable.

Mr. Schmitt was smiling. "Well, look who's here—in my favorite section, too. Didn't mean to bonk you in the nose like that!" He gave her shoulder an awkward pat.

Laurel was too embarrassed to respond.

"Are you okay?" Mr. Schmitt asked. "Anything I can help you with?"

Laurel shook her head hard. She turned away. Then something turned her around again. She looked at Mr. Schmitt. He was still smiling. He looked as if he was truly glad to see her.

"I know this sounds crazy," Laurel said. "But do you think there's any way a human brain could ever directly link up to a computer?"

Mr. Schmitt fixed a narrowed gaze on Laurel. "It does not sound crazy." He was speaking slowly and carefully. "It could happen. It *will* happen. Look at this." He led Laurel over to a stack of magazines. He flipped through one quickly and then pointed to a headline.

NEW TECHNOLOGY CAN TRANSMIT DATA THROUGH HUMAN BODY, the headline said. The article described how data had been sent from one man to another just by a handshake. One man held a transmitting device that sent the information through him to the other person using the human body's own natural electrical current. In the future, the developers said, the device would allow users to directly exchange data from electronic devices with other human beings.

Laurel pictured herself shaking hands with David Holyfield and instantaneously downloading computer files. "Can this stuff really be happening?" she marveled.

Mr. Schmitt's eyes had a slightly crazed glimmer. "Absolutely. People hooking directly into computers—it's just a question of when. Look, here's a cover story about a computer scientist who surgically implanted a chip in his arm that signaled his location to a computer network. Next he says he's going to implant a chip that can read signals directly from his nervous system and link them to a computer."

Now Mr. Schmitt was in full lecture mode. "Mind and Machine will be interchangeable. Don't take my word for it, though. Listen to Bill Gates, the guy who founded Microsoft. That's the most successful software company in history. In one interview I read, Bill Gates talked about how all the neurons in the brain—all the stuff that produces our feelings and perceptions—operate in a binary fashion. He said it's only a matter of time before computers will be able to hold the contents of the human brain. For all we know, some of these cutting-edge, secret-research types may already be there."

Some of these cutting-edge, secret-research types may already be there.... The thought of Mr. Holyfield, software developer, flashed through Laurel's mind.

But she still had lots of questions. "How exactly do you figure this kind of exchange could happen? I mean, a brain connecting directly with a computer. I mean, *how* would they communicate, and I don't know, I think I read that the electronic impulses a brain uses have a slower speed than computers."

"Yes, yes, brains and computers have different data speeds, but that can be easily corrected!"

Mr. Schmitt's voice was excited and loud—too loud, really, because heads were turning in their direction. "The other differences in the data sources could be corrected, too! You'd just need some special software to sort out the inconsistencies."

Some special software! So it could happen. Maybe David Holyfield really *had* hooked up directly to a computer. Again Laurel flashed on the mysterious Mr. Holyfield.

It was possible. The whole thing was possible. Bill Gates himself had said so.

As she waited for Jeanie, ready to ride home, these amazing concepts churned in Laurel's head.

Could Mind really meld with Machine?

Could a soul be stored on a hard drive?

And could you fall in love with software?

Laurel had actually been waiting for Jeanie quite a while. But excited as she felt, she wasn't in a hurry. Resentment, impatience, anger—all that had washed away. Instead, as Laurel now looked at scraggly-haired Jeanie struggling with her bike helmet, Laurel remembered the scene in the bathroom, and her heart filled with that tender, achy feeling again.

That evening Laurel watched her father use his computer. He'd agreed to show her how to use a program called TODO, which he described as an "overall search engine." TODO made it possible to do a systematic search of a PC's contents—every individual text file.

Dr. Shade turned the computer on and they waited for the main screen, where rows of brightly colored icons were arrayed. As Laurel watched, a couple of the icons squirmed, as if trying to escape their two-dimensional prison.

Laurel gasped. "They look like they're alive!"

Dr. Shade smiled in a pretend sinister way. He waggled his eyebrows.

Laurel's mother looked up from her gardening magazine.

"Laurel. Hold on a minute." She was speaking in a let's-get-things-straight voice. "Nothing in that computer is alive. I mean, yes, those little pictures dance around, but they aren't real like you and I are real. They're just images on the screen. Streams of electrons have instructions to make them dance."

Laurel thought about everything Computer Dave and Mr. Schmitt had said, about what her own library research had confirmed. "But, Mom, electrons make *us* dance, too. They control us, too. We're just a big collection of electrons. Electronic impulses go back and forth from our brain to the rest of our body, and that's what makes us do what we do and feel what we feel. I'm not sure you can say that people are more real than computers."

Dr. Shade was looking at Laurel with raised eyebrows. Then, slowly, he began clapping. "Well, well, well. I'm just amazed, to tell you the truth."

"I'm just confused," Mrs. Shade said. "To tell you the truth." She returned to her magazine.

I'm going to remember this day, Laurel thought as she lay in bed that night. *It's the day everything changed.*

Just then a whisper came from Jeanie's bed.

"Laurel?"

"What?"

"You know, I really love you."

Everything really *had* changed. Wow. Then the whisper rose again.

"Laurel?"

"Yes, Jeanie?"

"Did you remember that today was Opposite Day?"

A low, exasperated growl swelled inside Laurel. Someday someone was going to strangle that Jeanie.

chapter 15

Roberta lets out a small gasp when she opens the door and sees Laurel. Then she smiles. "Right on time for piano lesson," Roberta says in a Russian accent. "Come in, comrade!"

Wow, Laurel thinks. *This is definitely a new side of Roberta—a kind of goofy side.*

Then Roberta looks slightly sheepish and returns to her usual voice: "Just kidding. I'm really glad you came over. What would *you* like to do?"

"I want to do a global search—for your brother!"

Laurel tells Roberta about the global search concept, and shows her the diskette with the search engine program, TODO. She suggests they install it on the computer Roberta's brother used.

Roberta looks thoughtful. Then she nods. "Okey-dokey," she says, again evoking Great-uncle Walter.

She points Laurel to a computer at the end of the long table, the same computer that her brother had been using the day before. Then Roberta sits down at the piano. She begins playing soft, wispy musical fragments, her head and shoulders leaning toward the keyboard.

★ ★ ★

The computer used by David Holyfield turned out to have a great deal of storage: not one but two twenty-gigabyte hard drives. Countless CD-ROMs had been loaded onto it. It held thousands of other files, loaded and downloaded from all sorts of places.

FIND WHAT? the TODO program asked. Ever so carefully, Laurel typed: D-A-V-I-D

Up came the results of her search request: over six hundred entries included DAVID, the computer said. Did Laurel wish to narrow the search? Laurel thought briefly, then typed HOLYFIELD in the search box, right after DAVID.

Only two entries this time. Laurel pulled up the first. An image of a delicate, pale, nude young man, carved of marble, appeared on the screen.

A small shock wave traveled through Laurel.

It was from an Art World program, part of an article titled "Establishing the Date of Michelangelo's *David*," by Andrew Headly and Phyllis Holyfield.

Wrong David.

The second entry was from a program called Sports Bytes. It was a profile of the world heavyweight boxing champion, Evander Holyfield. The story compared him to David in the Bible story of David and Goliath.

Wrong again. "Oh man," Laurel moaned.

Then she had an insight. The kind of global search she was doing could never work, she realized. It was misguided to be searching for a *word,* like *David.* DAVID and HOLYFIELD were just strings of characters—just names that people used to refer to *things.* Laurel was only instructing the computer to look for a particular string of characters. What she really wanted was the thing those characters referred to. And maybe TODO wasn't what she needed—her dad had said TODO could search through the text files, but what she wanted was probably not stored as text.

Rats. Maybe it made more sense to start by just looking for a big enough file.

She became vaguely aware that Roberta was now standing right behind her. "Do you know how I can find out which files are really big?" Laurel asked. She turned around.

It was not Roberta. It was Computer Dave.

Tiny tremors shot through Laurel.

He sat down next to the computer, right next to her. She wrapped her arms around herself to keep from quivering.

Computer Dave's silvery green eyes were fixed on the computer screen. "You need to check the file directories and search the data profiles of all the files," he said.

He began typing. The arch of his nose was so perfect it made her ache.

All of a sudden he was looking directly at her. Laurel had a quick sense, a glimpse, a premonition of something about to happen.... But then he turned away and was once again staring at the monitor.

On the screen, columns of numbers began streaming past. "There you are, Laurel."

That's the first time he's used my name, Laurel thought. But the silvery green eyes showed no feelings. And then he was gone, simply gone. Without a word. Totally detached.

So what would the real David be like? He would have feelings, for one thing. He would care about things. Maybe he would care about her.

She imagined him looking deep into her eyes. She imagined him touching her cheek. Oddly, she found herself flinching. Something about the picture was unsettling.

If only she could shut off these crazy thoughts! What were her feelings, anyway? If she arranged them into a poem, would they start making any more sense?

> *If I found out that you wanted me*
> *I wonder what I'd do?*
> *Would my heart sing out inside me?*
> *Or… would I run from you?*

Then Laurel shook her head back and forth, hard. *Snap out of it,* she told herself. She returned to the search.

That day in the gym, Roberta had said that something happened to her brother right after they had moved to Chestnut Knoll. Laurel now pressed her for details, and Roberta told her that the Holyfields had moved to Chestnut Knoll in late July or early August. To be safe, Laurel decided to look at all the files that had been created or modified from July through mid-September.

How big would the file need to be? Laurel tried figuring. The amount of information contained in a human brain was astronomical, she remembered—something like a hundred trillion connections. Thanks to Jeanie's ape book, she'd realized that it wouldn't all need to be stored—only that tiny fraction that made a person himself. But even so, the file would have to be much bigger than anything Laurel was finding. She wondered if several different files could have been used.

She was beginning to feel slightly desperate. She was getting a scary idea about short-term computer memory, vanishing memory, RAM—random-access memory—that she didn't even want to put into words.

Bing-bing! sounded the doorbell.

Roberta jerked. Laurel whirled toward the door. A muffled voice came from outside. "Is Laurel Shade in there?"

Yikes! Who on earth could it be? Laurel wondered wildly. Then an image of Shannon, her nose crinkled up in a smile, flashed into Laurel's head. She cringed.

Roberta turned toward her with a searching look. *There's noth-*

ing to be afraid of, Laurel tried to remind herself, but a sheen of perspiration had already broken over her face.

Bing-bing!

Why did Shannon seem so determined to track her down? What would it be like to confront her here? "Maybe we could just not answer that," Laurel heard herself whisper.

Bing-bing! Bing-bing! "Open the door!" the muffled voice commanded. Roberta clapped her hands over her face, distressed.

Abruptly the door flew open. There stood Jeanie. Her mouth was tight with impatience, and she had one hand on her hip.

"Jeez, Jeanie, that's so rude." Laurel used a scolding tone, but actually felt relieved. "You shouldn't go around throwing other people's doors open like that."

"I had *no choice*—Mom told me to find you," Jeanie said.

"Come on in," Roberta said politely.

"I already am in," Jeanie said.

Roberta floundered only briefly. "So... um... would you like to sit down?"

"I wouldn't mind using your bathroom. I'm starting to feel a little bit like a star."

Roberta looked puzzled. "Like a *star*?"

"They're made out of gas, aren't they? So which way is the bathroom, anyway?"

"It's this way," said a monotone voice.

It was Computer Dave. He had materialized once more. Where did he come from when he appeared so suddenly, and where did he go when he vanished?

After the bathroom door had closed behind her, Jeanie started singing. She sang to herself, but the words of her song were plain.

> *"Twinkle, twinkle, little star,*
> *Pass your gas but stay up far."*

"Stop it, Jeanie!" Laurel heard her own voice rising louder than the singing, but Jeanie continued.

> *"When I hear your lonely fart,*
> *It's enough to break my heart...."*

Mortified, Laurel glanced at Roberta and her brother. Her voice rose almost to a shriek. "Jean-NEEY! WE DON'T SAY... that word... in this family!"

There was a brief pause. "Okay, Laurel," Jeanie called back. "What's a polite word for *fart?*"

Long silence. Laurel racked her brain. There had to be a polite word, but nothing came to mind. "Cut the cheese?" she finally offered weakly.

"Fine," Jeanie responded from the other side of the bathroom door.

> *"When I hear you cut the cheese,*
> *It's enough to make me sneeze...."*

"Your sister's quite a character," Roberta observed mildly.

When Jeanie emerged from the bathroom, she looked around, unsmiling. She settled herself into the nearest chair. Then she squinched her eyes shut. "Somehow I'm really in the mood for the Outer Space Channel now."

A tired feeling came over Laurel. She didn't feel angry, just tired. "So why did Mom want you to find me, anyway, Jeanie?"

"She wanted me to try to get you for lunch, and I thought you might be here. Now shush! They're showing some new video from the Hubble telescope."

Laurel stole a glance at Computer Dave. He was staring at Jeanie. His face looked somehow different than usual.

What *was* that change in his face? It bothered Laurel.

Ever so lightly, something touched her arm. She looked up and into Roberta's concerned eyes. Then Roberta smiled. It was not a mocking smile but a smile with understanding in it, an understanding that seemed to go down layers and layers and layers.

As Laurel looked at Roberta, she found herself thinking, *She's really so cute.*

Then she saw the man behind Roberta.

It was a man with black-framed glasses. He was standing in the doorway, one hand on the doorjamb.

Laurel's whole body jerked.

The man cleared his throat. "Everything okay?"

"Yes, Daddy," Roberta murmured.

This was the man who had cut down the climbing tree.

If Laurel had been asked what she'd feel the first time she saw this man, she could only have guessed. Indignation? Rage? Curiosity? She would never have predicted this terror. It was huge. It blasted through her body and pressed her toward the door.

She could not look at the man directly. It was physically impossible.

Instead, with wild eyes, she looked over at Jeanie. She saw her sister's face, warlike, screwing up, preparing to spew out some outrageous remark.

Riding a tidal wave of adrenaline, Laurel grabbed Jeanie by one arm and dragged her out the door. "We were just leaving," she called over her shoulder.

chapter 16

Dr. Shade arrives looking for lunch just moments after Laurel and Jeanie. He drops a paper in front of Laurel. "Thought you might be interested," he says. It's a photocopy of a magazine article: HOW IBM BUILT THE COMPUTER THAT BEAT THE WORLD CHESS CHAMP, says the headline.

"The line between computers and people is definitely blurring," Dr. Shade says. "Computers have been beating us at chess for quite a while now. Some people say, so what, the computer still isn't *thinking*—it's just making millions of electronic connections. But can we really say that when our brains think, they're doing anything different?"

Laurel's own brain has drifted, though—drifted back to Roberta. She's trying to imagine not having a mother. And she can't, not really. And she's trying to imagine having a father who's strange and terrifying and gone all the time. So all you really have is your brother, and then your brother's mind gets lost in a computer somehow.

Laurel vows to go back to Roberta's house right after lunch—terror or no terror.

When her brain drifts back to the kitchen, Laurel sees her

mother watching her intently. "Are you planning to disappear again after lunch?" her mother says. Her voice has that edgy sound.

"I'm going over to a friend's house."

Mrs. Shade narrows her eyes. "Which friend are we talking about?"

"A new kid. She lives right near here." A pause; her mother's eyes are still narrowed. "Roberta something."

"Roberta Holyfield?" Mrs. Shade says unexpectedly.

Laurel feels sheepish. "Yeah, I think that's her name."

Mrs. Shade raises her eyebrows ever so slightly.

When Laurel got back to the Holyfields', there was no sign of either the father or the brother. Roberta ushered her inside with a grateful look. But when Laurel hurried over to David's computer, Roberta's face clouded.

She must be worried sick about her brother, Laurel thought, and made up her mind to console her. "Listen, Roberta. I want to promise you something. I promise I'm going to do everything I can to get your real brother back. And I bet we can do it—you and me together."

Roberta gave her a wan smile.

"But you know, there *is* one thing I'm really worried about," Laurel said.

She confessed her fears about RAM. RAM, she had read, was a computer's basic operational memory. It had speed and flexibility, but it was strictly short-term. It held information only as long as electrical current was flowing through the computer. When the computer was turned off, everything in RAM just disappeared. So anything you wanted to save had to be stored—converted to some other way of recording binary information, like magnetism, that didn't depend on electrical current.

"So here's what keeps worrying me," Laurel said. "What if David's brain was in RAM and *never got stored*? What if his mind kind of got dumped into nothingness when the computer was turned off?"

Roberta let out a tortured-sounding sigh.

Laurel replayed her own words. They were chilling. She felt terrible. What a thing to spill out—and she was supposed to be consoling Roberta! She looked down at her lap, appalled at her own insensitivity. Why hadn't she kept her mouth shut about this RAM thing?

There was an awkward silence. Eventually Roberta began speaking in a subdued voice. "Look, I'm not an expert, but I don't think you need to worry about that. Maybe with some older computers, but not with any of ours. My dad said any unsaved data is automatically written to the hard drive before the computer is turned off. And then, see, like this computer you're using"—Roberta reached over and typed briefly—"it's set for a three-minute save. So whenever you work on anything for three minutes or more, the computer automatically makes a permanent file on the hard drive, or the diskette, whichever, and then updates it every three minutes."

Roberta herself had already put the RAM fears to rest! What a relief. In the search for her brother, she had obviously thought about this possibility and then ruled it out.

But right now Roberta seemed preoccupied. She was fingering the piano keys. "I think you should try *this* keyboard for a while," she finally said with a flicker of a smile.

"What's that music you're playing now?"

"Nothing. Just something I made up." Roberta sounded embarrassed.

"You're kidding. You didn't tell me you wrote real music!"

Roberta smiled. Behind the glasses her eyes looked pixielike, and her skin stretched over her cheeks. Her skin was so tan—though *tan* didn't seem like a very good word for it. The color was more like honey, or maybe amber.

"Do you write your music down?" Laurel asked.

"Oh no, it's not a big deal."

"Yes it is. You *should* write it down. You have to!"

Roberta smiled again and went to get a pad of paper. Laurel felt secretly pleased at how nice she was being to Roberta.

Roberta drew five parallel lines across the paper and then started filling them with musical notes. "That's it, that's what I was just playing." At the top of the page, she wrote: "Song for Laurel."

"Wow. Nobody's ever written a song for me before."

"What about your little sister? She ought to dedicate her new version of 'Twinkle, Twinkle, Little Star' to you. After all, you really deserve credit for that part about cutting the cheese."

Roberta was struggling to look serious. She failed. Then they were both roaring with laughter.

"But you know, there was something kind of touching about her version of 'Twinkle, Twinkle,'" Roberta said after a minute. "I mean, poor star. So full of gas! And so lonely it breaks your heart."

Laurel just smiled and rolled her eyes. She looked again at "Song for Laurel." The musical notes reminded her of children chasing one another, some holding hands, some with fluttering hair. She took the pencil and started adding feet and clothing and smiles. Then Laurel got really enthusiastic. She drew a new set of lines and sprinkled them with her own dancing note-children.

"Well, well, well. You didn't tell me *you* wrote music," Roberta said. "Would you like to hear the song you just wrote?"

She played a few notes. It didn't sound like a real song, not really. In spite of herself, Laurel felt a little disappointed.

Roberta hadn't given up, though. "You know, if we repeat that, it's not bad." She played the notes again, twice, and then penciled in a fat pair of dots, one above the other, at the end of Laurel's dancing children. "That's the sign that tells you to repeat the notes."

"But now my kids look like they're being chased by a couple of bumblebees! Someone save those poor kids!"

They began roaring with laughter all over again.

I seem wittier than usual, Laurel thought. *I feel like some new and better version of myself.*

Then a harsh throat-clearing noise crackled across the room. "Excuse me. Roberta."

It was the man with the black-framed glasses. Roberta's father. Once again he was standing in the doorway.

Questions—accusations—galloped through Laurel's head: *Why did you cut down the climbing tree? And what's happened to your son?* Strangely, though, this time there was no blinding terror. It must have spent itself.

She was able to look at his face now. He was middle-aged, of medium height, with thinning brownish hair—nondescript, really, except for the black-framed glasses. His manner was distracted. When Roberta introduced him to Laurel, he barely glanced her way.

He was saying that he had business calls to make and maybe the girls could play outside. It was a nice day, he said.

And it *was* a nice day outside, a beautiful day actually. Clear. Perfect temperature. Crisp autumn smell. As they stood in the yard, they breathed deeply, taking in the afternoon.

High overhead, they heard a sudden rustling and a cawing—a strong breeze had stirred the treetops, startling the birds. Something about that breeze, with its autumn smell, was thrilling. It made Laurel feel adventurous.

"Let's go someplace! Maybe we could go to Cleve's!"

Roberta looked awkward.

"What's the matter?" Laurel prodded. "Look, we don't have to go to Cleve's if you don't want to."

"I don't know who that is," Roberta finally mumbled. "Or what that is."

Roberta had never been to Cleve's. She had never even heard of Cleve's. In that moment Laurel saw the full depth of the

Holyfields' isolation. To have never heard of Cleve's, never gone there with a friend—why, you'd have to be totally excluded from Chestnut Knoll life. Totally… cast out.

Just like you'll be, said a voice inside Laurel, *if anyone sees you with this kid. You walk to Cleve's with Roberta, you're an outcast, too—a weirdo.*

But just then the breeze swelled up again, fluttering Laurel's hair and filling her with courage. She looked at Roberta's small, earnest face and put her hands on her shoulders.

"We're going to Cleve's," Laurel said. After all, she reminded herself with a small smile, *weirdo* meant something really good in Turbish.

Oddly, they didn't see a soul on the walk to Cleve's, and the store was empty when they got there. Laurel felt tensed for a thunderclap but did her best to act carefree. She and Roberta drifted down the aisles. Laurel showed Roberta the awesome expanse of the candy counter.

Cleve called over from behind the cash register. "You know something, Lovely Laurel? I don't think I've met your friend."

Laurel gave him an uneasy smile.

"Does she have a name?" Cleve prodded.

Other sounds filled the store just then. Several sixth-grade girls from Tuckerman had come into Cleve's and were talking gaily.

The group included Sarah Teller. She spotted Laurel and started to say something. Then she noticed Roberta. Sarah's eyes widened.

"Hi, Sarah," Laurel said, her heart whirring.

Sarah didn't answer. She turned her back on Laurel and began buzzing to the other girls.

"Oh my God," someone groaned. Heat flashed to Laurel's cheeks.

Another voice, artificially high and nasal, called out, "Emergency! Clear the store!" The group ran outside, squealing.

Quiet began to drift back over the store.

Then Cleve cleared his throat. "Before we were so *rudely* interrupted," he said, "I was angling for an introduction."

Laurel hesitated. She was remembering the petition that Cleve had organized about the climbing tree. She looked at Cleve's wide face. He smiled at the two of them, and then gave Laurel a reassuring wink. Gratitude overwhelmed her. Oh Cleve. He was so understanding. He was wonderful.

Cleve nodded in Roberta's direction. "Pleased to meet you, Madame X."

Laurel had to laugh. "This is my friend Roberta. Roberta, this is Cleve."

Roberta, looking tiny and shy, shook Cleve's hand.

A question had meanwhile occurred to Laurel. "I can't believe I don't know this. Is Cleve your first name or your last name?"

"Neither."

"*What?*"

"Neither, I said."

"Then why does everyone call you that?"

"I guess they don't know any better."

Laurel began to suspect that Cleve was having fun with her. She searched his face for some hint of a smile. "Then why is this store called Cleve's?" she finally burst out.

"Bought it from a man named Cleve," he answered. "Guy was a real piece of work, too. Chestnut Knoll is lucky to be rid of that character."

This was a startling development, a little like being told that the first month of the year wasn't really called January. It would take a while to settle in.

"So what *is* your name?" Laurel asked, almost as an afterthought.

"Les. Les Somers."

"I'd like *more* summers," Roberta said.

"You and me both!" said Cleve/Les Somers with a chuckle.

Outside of Cleve's, some boys had joined up with Sarah Teller's group. When Laurel saw them, her body almost jerked her back into the store. *I don't wanna, I don't wanna,* a voice sang crazily inside her. She chided herself. *Come on. Get a grip. You were going to be the kind of kid who'd stand up to Nazis!* Okay, so this was just some stupid bunch of sixth graders. But to walk out there with Roberta now—well, that counted for something, too.

She tried calling up the memory of the earlier breeze, how it had filled her with a spirit of adventure. She lifted her chin. She put her hand on Roberta's elbow and led her outside.

Laurel squinted in the afternoon sun. Then she forced her eyes over to the sidewalk crowd. She smiled mechanically in their direction and murmured, "Hi, everyone" as she led Roberta past.

Laurel and Roberta had almost reached the corner before anyone responded.

"What's your problem, Shade?" a voice said loudly. "How can you be friends with that kid?"

"This kid," Laurel began; her voice was all wrong, high-pitched and quivery. "This… *kid*… didn't do anything!"

"They cut down the climbing tree!" someone called.

Laurel started to answer, but a feeling of pointlessness overcame her. She glanced at Roberta, who looked like she wanted to slide into a sidewalk crack. So Laurel tightened her grip on Roberta's arm and started walking again.

At the corner, she nudged Roberta down the side street. *Tuckerman is sure buzzing now,* she thought. *And we didn't even have school today.*

A few more steps and something cracked inside her.

"Roberta. This really stinks."

Laurel stopped walking. Her eyes started to sting. Then acid tears were spilling down her cheeks.

She clapped her hands over her face. Where had these tears been storing themselves that they now pushed out with such force?

She flopped herself down on the hood of a sleek red parked car.

Wup.

The air vibrated with the strange noise. Laurel jumped back up.

Wup-wup, the sound continued. It was getting louder. It seemed to be surrounding them. *Wup-wup. WUP-WUP!*

Roberta cupped her hands around Laurel's ear. "Car alarm."

The sound was earsplitting. *WUP-WUP-WUP-WUP-WUP-WUP…*

An odd energy started to pump through Laurel. "Let's get out of here!"

Immediately they were pounding down the street, then turning and pounding down an alley. At the end of the alley they stopped. The *wupping* continued, but now it sounded far away.

Laurel's heart was banging, and her breath came in gasps. She flung herself down on a low brick wall. Then she jumped up again, nervous, and looked wild-eyed at Roberta.

Roberta smiled. "I don't think there are any alarms *here.*"

Laurel began to giggle. A small white dog peered through the metal slats of a chain-link fence and gave her a questioning bark.

Laurel could not get control of the giggling. She sucked in a big breath, trying to calm herself, but it made a croaky, wheezy sound. The dog's bark became accusing.

"Uh-oh," said Roberta. "Looks like we did set off another alarm." This comment triggered a loud, shrieky laugh from Laurel.

The dog's bark was piercing now—shattering. He began hurling himself against the fence. Laurel still couldn't stop laughing.

Now the dog was backing up, taking a running start. He catapulted himself toward them, smashing into the fence, causing a shattering sound and a violent ripple that ran down the entire expanse of fence.

A man's voice boomed out of nowhere. *"Shut up, Hannibal! What's going on out there?"*

So once again the girls were running, this time back up the

alley. Laurel was laughing too much to hold herself straight. She had to scuttle along in a ridiculous half-crouch.

They ran down a side street, then another. Somehow they ended up on Boulder Street, which led to Saxon Lane, Laurel's street. They didn't stop running till they were in Laurel's backyard. Then they collapsed on the grass and gasped for breath.

Laurel listened to her heart, still banging in her chest. She stretched her arms out over her head. She breathed in that autumn-smelling breeze and watched shaggy white clouds blow across the sky. She wondered vaguely if the little scratchy feeling on her ankle was a piece of grass or some insect.

Roberta spoke the first words since the bark attack. "Holy smoke."

"Holy cow," Laurel offered in response.

"Holy Toledo!"

Laurel thought briefly. "Holy Pittsburgh!"

The phrase was intended in honor of Roberta. But Roberta did not look honored. Instead, she sat up abruptly. Her face seemed to be crumbling.

Uh-oh—not the right thing to say, obviously. Laurel felt bad. She rolled over and propped her head up. "Does it make you sad, thinking about when you lived in Pittsburgh?"

Roberta took off her glasses and rubbed the bridge of her nose. "No," she answered. She put her glasses back on and stared off into the distance. "I never lived in Pittsburgh."

Oh *man*. Laurel was stunned. "So where did you live before this?"

"We lived in a tiny little town near Gettysburg, Pennsylvania."

"Like Chestnut Knoll?"

"No." Roberta's voice had a straining sound. "Definitely *not* like Chestnut Knoll." Then a miserable lump of silence hung between them.

Change the subject. Quick.

Laurel began spurting words. "Sometimes I write poetry, at least I try. It's not very good or anything, but it's sort of fun, or maybe not exactly fun but… I don't know, something about it feels good." She sounded like she was babbling. "You start off not knowing what you're going to say and then you end up saying something. But not always." Oh man, she actually *was* babbling. But if she stopped, Roberta was going to cry or something, and they'd had enough tears for one day. "Anyway, maybe I'll write a poem about that trip home. I think it's good material for a poem. Very intense."

"Very alarming," said Roberta.

A delighted laugh rose from Laurel. She laughed it extra loud to drive off any remaining misery. There was something soft and stealthy about Roberta's sense of humor, she thought. It kind of tiptoed up on you.

That trip home *had* been alarming, and intense, and horrible in places. But it had also been fun. Laurel pictured the white dog in the alley and Roberta saying, "Looks like we did set off another alarm." Wait a minute—play back that tape. She didn't say *you,* Laurel realized, she said *we.*

They lay back on the grass and watched clouds for a while. Then a strange impulse took hold of Laurel. "You know, there used to be this very cool… place."

Something had made her want to talk to Roberta about the climbing tree. But then she pictured Roberta's face starting to crumble again, and the words dried up in her mouth. "Anyway, it was kind of a cool place. I'll have to tell you about it sometime."

"You'll never believe this," Laurel told Jeanie that night. "Cleve's name isn't really Cleve. It's Les Somers."

"I knew that," Jeanie said. Then, after a minute: "Why does everyone call him Cleve?"

Laurel snorted. "I thought you knew everything! Because the guy he bought the store from was named Cleve. So it was the name of the store."

Jeanie didn't say anything.

"And guess what? The Holyfields aren't from Pittsburgh. They're from some teensy little town in Pennsylvania. And don't tell me you knew that, too."

Jeanie just sniffed. When she spoke again, her voice was sulky. "Well, since *you're* such a genius, I'm sure you've managed to find David in the computer by now."

David—and the computer—Laurel hadn't thought about that for hours! Now she burst into chatter. "You know, Jeanie, I'm really starting to get a picture of how computers work, and how similar they are to brains. But I can't figure out what kind of fluke would get them mixed. What mistake could David have made?"

Jeanie turned and stared. Her face was puckered with exasperation.

"Don't you get it—it's the father!" she hissed. "He messed with his son's brain somehow. *He's a software developer, for crying out loud!*"

Well, there it was, stated in plain English. "Come on, Jeanie," Laurel said uneasily. "Do you really think a father could do a thing like that to his son?"

"Hey, you two, no more talking," Mrs. Shade called sharply. "Jeanie, you should have been asleep an hour ago! School tomorrow."

At the mention of school, the reality of Laurel's own situation came back to her. Yuck. Double yuck. School tomorrow.

Laurel decided she'd arrive as late as possible. She'd get there on Aubrey Madison time.

chapter 17

After a long night of tossing, Laurel wakes up unnaturally early. She's got the shivers.

Just hanging around the house feels like torture. So she decides that instead of getting to school on Aubrey Madison time, she'll tell her mother she needs to go in early.

Mrs. Shade wants to know why.

"To see Mr. Schmitt, the computer science teacher," Laurel answers. And in that very instant, she decides that she really does want to talk to him.

There were many reasons for computer file mix-ups, according to Mr. Schmitt. He said he couldn't answer Laurel's question without looking at the computer with the problem. Viruses were a big source of trouble, he added, and asked if the file mix-up was a recurring problem. Laurel said she didn't think so.

"If you want to run a complete virus check, let me know. I have some software that could help you." Mr. Schmitt looked up at the ceiling, thinking. "Just off the top of my head, I can think of one other way that files can get exchanged. Especially with an older computer, or maybe with some flaky new component. The problem has to do with the interrupt."

A computer's different components—its parts, like the keyboard, mouse, monitor, sound card, video card—all needed to communicate with the central processing unit, called the CPU. The CPU was sort of like the computer's brain. Most of the components communicated with the CPU by sending a particular type of signal called an *interrupt*. The interrupt told the CPU to stop what it was doing and respond to that particular component's request.

"Each interrupt gets assigned a certain code. In newer computer components there's usually a standardized protocol for assigning the codes. But a computer could get set up so that, by mistake, two components use the exact same interrupt code. Then the CPU wouldn't be able to tell which device was asking for attention," Mr. Schmitt explained. "That's called a conflict. And it's the reason behind some really bizarre computer glitches."

He was not quite in lecture mode, but edging closer by the minute. His eyes were getting that slightly crazed glimmer. "The point is, with a conflict, you just can't predict the outcome. Here's an example, okay? Imagine one component is telling the CPU to put something in memory. And then maybe a second component is telling the CPU to... oh, let's say, to scan something. If the two components use the same interrupt, I think maybe the computer could end up putting the wrong thing in memory."

If several computers were networked together, things could get even more complicated, he added. "Does the site you're talking about have more than one computer?"

"Yes," Laurel said. "Maybe six. Not counting the laptops."

"Sheesh," said Mr. Schmitt.

Laurel started playing out various scenarios in her mind: Assume it was some accident, something innocent. Assume David had been directly linked to the computer. Assume he had sent the

CPU some unknown command, using an interrupt with a particular code. And then another command was made, using the same interrupt code and telling the CPU to... what? To store something in memory? So some part of David had been stored in memory instead. A conflict.

But wait. Suppose for a minute that David *had* gotten caught in a conflict and had gotten stored or something. In that case a part of his brain had been written to the computer. But something had also taken its place, right? Some computer data had also been written to *his* brain.

"When you send data someplace, and something else replaces it, does it have to happen at exactly the same time?" Laurel asked Mr. Schmitt.

"Wait a second, wait a second, *wait one second!* The data you transmit doesn't get up and go where you send it. It sends a signal that copies its own pattern of electrical pulses," Mr. Schmitt said. Now, Laurel saw, he was past the point of no return. He was fully in lecture mode.

"Same thing as the Internet. When you transmit data over the Internet, it doesn't leave your computer. What you send is an electronic signal that copies the pattern of pulses in your data and transmits them somewhere else. A little bit like sending a fax. You don't send off the original, it just gets electronically copied and transmitted. That's the beauty of this whole technology...."

Mr. Schmitt continued lecturing, but Laurel had tuned him out. So several steps were necessary. Part of David's brain had been written to the computer. But instead of just being copied, the original part must have been deleted from his brain. So was the crossed command a DELETE?

Laurel tried making diagrams in her head that would explain everything. But each scenario at some point seemed to collapse like a house of cards. She had to keep adding more and more layers, more steps, to account for it all.

How could such a complex sequence possibly be an accident? Then the shadow of the mysterious Mr. Holyfield seemed to loom over everything. Laurel recalled Jeanie's whispered comment the night before: *"Don't you get it—it's the father!"* Surely he couldn't have done something like that to his own son on purpose. Yet how else could you explain this complicated chain of computer events? It just couldn't be accidental. And after all, this was the man who had cut down the climbing tree. Who knew what went on in that mind?

Laurel got to her classroom just as the bell rang, only a heartbeat ahead of Aubrey Madison.

Several of her classmates were still gathered at the classroom door. Laurel's stomach fluttered, and her head jerked down before she could stop it. The other kids greeted her with silence. Then came a small burst of titters and snickers.

Laurel sat down and fixed her eyes on her desktop. After a few minutes she realized she was holding her breath. And improbably, ridiculously, Jeanie's version of "Twinkle, Twinkle, Little Star" was playing somewhere in the back of her head.

She looked at the Holyfield boy in profile. A miserable yearning swelled inside. Oh *why* was she so drawn to him? If only her heart could have picked a regular kid—one with regular feelings. What was she supposed to do with her feelings for him? *He* had no use for them.

She was doing such crazy things now, partly for him, and he didn't care. He didn't want her. He didn't want anybody.

How could she explain this yearning, even to herself? What was it, exactly, about him?

> *How I wonder what you are,*
> *You solitary friend of none.*

I thought that you might be my star.
Now somehow I'm the lonely one.

Self-pity rose in a great wave, but she pushed it back ferociously. She *would* get through the morning.

When she walked into the lunchroom, Laurel refused to let herself even glance at her usual lunch table, where Chrissie and Sarah Teller sat. Instead, she marched to an empty table across the room. She wondered who would join her. Every chair was needed at lunchtime, so someone had to sit next to her.

There was no point in looking for the Holyfield boy, of course. He was never in the lunchroom. If only Roberta had lunch at the same time. Unfortunately Laurel's class ate during the first lunch period and Roberta's didn't eat until the third—though they would at least have recess together during the second period.

It didn't really matter who sat at her table. Anyone could sit there. What a ridiculous thing to care about, Laurel thought, remembering her past snobbery.

No one sat at Laurel's table.

Someone has to sit here, she thought. *The tables are always full at lunch!* She began to feel slightly frantic.

"Whatsa matta, Laurel?" someone was saying. "What are you doing all by yourself?"

Laurel looked up in gratitude. It was Mrs. T, one of the lunchroom monitors. Her face was crinkled with concern.

Laurel started to answer but found her throat clogging and her eyes stinging dangerously. She bolted out the lunchroom door.

The playground stretched out before her. And there, off in the distance—it was Roberta! Her class had come out early for recess. She was sitting alone on the same low wall where Laurel had first approached Yuriko. Roberta looked as breakable as a twig.

She was so, so far away. She was on the far side of hostile territory. Laurel sucked in her breath and pushed up her chin, trying to look fearless, and began moving toward her.

It was a long, slow slog. A walk through molasses. She walked past the cliques and the clusters—past the card traders, the boxballers, the gymnasts, the gossips—all staring at her coolly. Laurel's feet had forgotten how long each step should be. And what were her hands supposed to do while the rest of her was walking?

At last she reached Roberta. She sat down next to her. Roberta gave her a winsome smile, and Laurel's spirits soared. Immediately, a voice called out across the blacktop, shouting something about a "tree killer" next to "the Shade."

The remark stung a little, but Laurel kept her eyes on Roberta's eyes. This was how to prevent motion sickness, she recalled—keep your eyes on the one fixed point you can find.

Roberta stretched her thin legs out over the blacktop. She said she had an idea. "I was thinking about what you said about writing poetry. Just think. You like to write poetry and I like to write music. Maybe we could be a songwriting team. You do the words, I do the music."

"Cool! What should our first song be about?"

"Well, let's see. Hmmm. They say the best writing comes from your own experience. We could write a song about today. About right now." Roberta stared down at her outstretched legs. They looked as delicate as a colt's. "We could call it…" She paused. "We could call it 'Bad Day at Blacktop.'" She looked over at Laurel mischievously. Then she started humming something with a cowboy flavor.

Laurel had to smile. Out loud, she began composing rapidly.

The sky was gray, the wind was cold,
But Roberta and Laurel were feeling bold.

From Pennsylvania Roberta had come.
On her back was a piano, in her mouth was a hum.

"If you want to add anything, go right ahead," she told
Roberta.

"Can't right now, can't talk," mumbled Roberta. "In my mouth
is a hum." She looked at Laurel innocently. "And man, is my back
ever aching."

Laurel cracked up. "Okay, okay, it's still a little rough. I don't
usually compose this fast."

Amazing how safe it felt in this little corner of the blacktop.
When the bell rang and the playground began emptying, Laurel
turned toward the building with reluctance.

Aubrey Madison emerged from a dark car and floated toward
the school, smile going full dazzle. When her smile reached Laurel
and Roberta, Aubrey paused. She stared at them for a few seconds.

Briefly, a strange, intent look came over Aubrey's face. Then she
returned to transmitting the dazzling smile. She floated inside.

Time to go into the building, no getting around it. Even
Aubrey was ahead of them.

As Laurel moved toward the entrance to the school, she found
herself caught up in a sea of students. Someone touched her arm.
It was Chrissie Paradiso, with betrayed-looking eyes. "Laurel,
they're saying you wanted the climbing tree cut down so you'd
have room near your yard for a tetherball. Is that really true?"

Laurel stared at Chrissie, thunderstruck. Then the sea of students seemed to pull Chrissie away, still looking back at Laurel
with those betrayed eyes. Chrissie's lips were moving, but Laurel
couldn't hear the words anymore.

When the bell rang at the end of the day and the students flowed
into the hall, dread tugged briefly at Laurel. But she put on an

expressionless mask and strode into the crowd. She was getting better at this outcast thing, she decided.

The crowd moved toward the door at the end of the hall. *Careful now, here comes that scratchy part of the wall.*

Yikes! The crowd of bodies seemed to force her over to the side. A panicky feeling surged up. She felt a vague pressure, and then a definite shove. Her left elbow scraped against cement, and pain blazed up her arm.

A pig-snorting sound followed. Laurel twisted and saw Shannon right next to her. Shannon stared coolly into her eyes. Laurel looked away, cheeks hot, the skin on her elbow burning. Again she heard the pig snort.

You were my friend, Laurel thought. *Or were you? Were you ever?*

Misery began oozing up from some secret well inside, gradually filling her, almost oozing out her eyes. She stumbled toward the light at the end of the hall and stepped outside.

Her mother was there. Mrs. Shade was standing at the top of the steps. She was waiting at the spot where they used to meet when Laurel was too young to walk home alone.

Was this really happening?

"The car's over this way, Laurel," Mrs. Shade called in a commanding voice. "Come on, we'll be late."

The crowd parted. Laurel rushed to her mother. Feelings of love and thankfulness overwhelmed her. But what on earth was her mother doing there? She almost never came to the school to pick Laurel up anymore. And what was it they were late for?

"Come on, we can't be late," Mrs. Shade said firmly. She looked majestic and somehow even taller than usual as she walked down the steps of the school. "Why don't you get those Holyfield kids, too. Roberta and… what's the boy's name? David?"

How could her mom know so much about the Holyfields?

152

And whatever was she doing there? Laurel was baffled. "Mom, how do you know all this stuff?"

"I'm your mother. I know everything." Not a very satisfying answer, but from the set of her mother's mouth it would have to do for now. A mysterious maternal radar seemed to be at work.

"Well at least tell me... are we taking Jeanie somewhere? What are we going to be late for?"

Her mother looked at Laurel briefly. "It's just a sort of figure of speech," she said primly. "Jeanie's carpooling with the Meyer boy to an after-school class. And I had some extra time today. You go get those kids and meet me at the car. It's right across the street."

As Laurel and Roberta climbed into the Shades' minivan, Roberta explained to Mrs. Shade that her brother had a chess club meeting after school every Tuesday.

"Oh really? Chess? Your brother plays chess?" Laurel's mother said. "That's interesting. You know, Jeanie's been saying she wants to learn chess. Right now she's at a tae kwon do lesson, so she'll be home a little later, too."

Jeanie at a tae kwon do lesson. Jeanie learning martial arts. Belatedly the idea snapped like a rubber band inside Laurel's head. "Tae kwon do? Jeanie?" She shuddered. "But *why*?"

"It's something she asked to do," Mrs. Shade said. In the background the car radio was playing a familiar song. Unexpectedly, Mrs. Shade began singing along in a loud voice. Then she executed a series of thumps on the steering wheel with the palm of her hand in time to the music.

When her drum performance was finished, Mrs. Shade glanced toward the backseat. "Roberta, would you and your brother like to go out to dinner? Once your brother gets back?" she asked abruptly. Roberta looked startled, then said yes.

"Well then, good. Let's check with your mom," Mrs. Shade said.

"It's just our dad. And he won't mind. He's gone till late. He told us to order pizza."

"Dr. Shade is out of town until late tonight, too," Laurel's mother said. "So that works out pretty well."

Laurel pictured herself in a restaurant with David Holyfield and felt a thrill. "As soon as Jeanie gets back, we'll all go," her mother continued, and the thrill faded. Having Jeanie around changed everything.

As they were pulling up to their house, Laurel had an inspiration. She whispered to Roberta that they ought to go to Roberta's house and work on their "project." Roberta looked delighted. When they asked Mrs. Shade, she said they could go for half an hour.

As soon as they reached the Holyfields' house, Roberta headed for the piano.

"No, wait, Roberta—don't get distracted! We should check that computer while we have a chance! I've got this idea about looking for compressed files. This is the perfect time—no one's around."

But Roberta looked positively deflated at Laurel's suggestion. She seemed to have lost all interest in the search. "I thought you wanted to work on our song," she said wistfully. "That's what I'm going to do." Her eyes had a worried look.

Laurel was torn. She was clearly disappointing Roberta; that felt bad. But Laurel was almost starting to wonder if Roberta had lost her perspective. Maybe she was getting too used to her aloneness. Maybe she needed her brother more than she remembered.

Laurel moved toward the brother's computer and sat down. She began hunting through its contents again with a renewed sense of urgency.

She pulled up file after file. She didn't know exactly what she was looking for but felt fairly sure she wasn't seeing it. "Do you know anything about data compression?" she asked.

Abruptly, Roberta banged a jarring chord on the piano. Then she stopped playing altogether. Her face looked tight. "No, I don't. Let's just go back to your house, Laurel. I don't want to be late. I'll just leave a note for my brother."

She is really *upset,* Laurel thought. Was Roberta starting to think they'd never get her brother back? Had Laurel done something wrong? Her insides felt twisted-up and unhappy.

On the walk back to the Shade house they didn't say a word. Laurel didn't really understand what was happening, but she knew she felt miserable. "I'm sorry, Roberta," she finally said awkwardly.

Roberta stopped walking and looked at her, eyebrows furrowed. "No! Don't say that. You haven't done anything."

Then a car pulled into the driveway. Jeanie was in the back seat, sitting next to a sullen-looking sandy-haired boy. "Hi, Mrs. Meyer! Hi, Sam! Hi, Jeanie!" Mrs. Shade's voice was ridiculously jolly. Then she asked, a little anxiously, "How did it go, kids?"

In response, the boy in the back seat blew a large bubble of spit.

Jeanie addressed her shoes in a fakey singsong voice. "Well, *thank* you so *much* for taking me." She climbed out of the car with a face like she'd just whiffed vinegar.

As usual, Jeanie set about capturing Nightshade as soon as she got into the house. She wrapped the helpless kitten around her neck like a fur stole. Then she sat down on the kitchen floor and pinned Nightshade under her folded legs. His tail twitched wildly.

"Let go of him—his tail is twitching," Laurel scolded. "That means he wants you to let go."

"No," Jeanie said flatly. "He's trying to send us a message. He's sending us a message in Cat Tail code."

"Cat Tail code?" Roberta repeated politely.

"Yes, Cat Tail code. Don't you ever watch the Kitten Channel? He's trying to warn us about something." Jeanie's voice was solemn, but her eyes glowed.

A weary sigh began to gather inside Laurel. But then somehow she found herself smiling. She turned toward Jeanie generously. "So what made you decide to learn Cat Tail code?"

"Just did," Jeanie answered. Then she scooped Nightshade into her arms and skipped away.

Out of the corner of her eye, Laurel suddenly saw Computer Dave. A thrill briefly convulsed her.

He was standing in the doorway looking in. He looked odd, his face altered in some way that Laurel couldn't quite name. His eyes were following Jeanie.

Then he turned toward Laurel. When he looked at her, those silvery green eyes seemed to jolt her with an electrical charge.

chapter 18

The five of them are having dinner at Lilacs: Laurel, Jeanie, Mrs. Shade, and the Holyfield kids. Everyone is sitting stiffly and keeping their eyes down while they wait for their food to arrive. Mrs. Shade is the only one talking. She's asking polite little questions. Then she seems to run out of ideas and no one says anything.

Eventually the silence is broken by agonized noises from the bottom of Jeanie's glass. She is sucking furiously at her straw. The sound is somewhere between a cement mixer and an injured elephant. Mrs. Shade pointedly ignores it for several minutes.

At last Mrs. Shade snaps. *"Don't suck like that!"*

Jeanie lifts her head and frowns. "I thought we didn't say 'sucks' in this family."

When the waiter finally put their steaming plates in front of them, Roberta's glasses fogged. Computer Dave immediately began transporting food to his mouth in quick, robotic movements. His eyes were riveted on his plate. As Laurel watched him, that familiar longing churned inside. But he didn't care, that was obvious. He didn't care in the least.

Jeanie also watched him for a minute. Then she spoke. "I want to ask you a question." Her eyes moved from Computer Dave to Roberta. "I want to know what happened to your mother."

Laurel was shocked. "Jeanie! Mind your own business!"

But Jeanie was undeterred. "And I also want to know some things about your dad."

Mrs. Shade jerked her head toward Jeanie. "Stop it right now! That is rude, that's inappropriate...."

Laurel simultaneously exploded. "Jeanie! You... little snot!"

"Hey. Don't call me snot, it's not polite," Jeanie said indignantly. She lifted her chin. "Call me... nasal mucus."

Laurel was momentarily paralyzed, torn between laughing and screaming. She ended up burying her head in her hands.

"Elbows off the table," said Jeanie. "That's not polite either. So anyway, you guys, what's the deal with your parents?"

Oh man. Jeanie's brashness was stunning. She approached these wrenching subjects with all the delicacy of an ax-murderer. Laurel felt slightly dazed. Then she became aware of Roberta's voice and realized that she had actually begun to answer Jeanie's questions.

Their mother had died of cancer, Roberta told Jeanie, three or four years earlier. She'd been a lawyer and the real breadwinner of the family. The father's software-development business had never made much money. So after their mother's death, to keep the bills paid, their dad had to put in a lot of extra hours and travel more. They'd moved to the New York area for his business.

Laurel looked hard at Roberta, and wondered if she'd ever really looked at her before. What was it like to be in those shoes, really in them? Earlier Laurel had tried to imagine not having a mother and had failed. The idea had just stayed flat. But to *have* a mother and watch her *die*—that thought was simply shattering.

And then to pack up and leave your home for a place that made you an outcast.

And Roberta never even acted sorry for herself.

Wasn't it just so incredibly peculiar, Laurel thought. All these deep secrets about Roberta, these things Laurel had longed to know and been too delicate to ask—they were gliding out now, one after another. Was it really so simple? Well, Laurel's old way of being sure didn't seem to work anymore. Maybe there was something to be said for just swinging a verbal ax like Jeanie.

Laurel looked over at her sister. She saw that Computer Dave was watching Jeanie, too. Once again, Laurel noticed, his eyes seemed to look different than usual. What *was* that peculiar expression? Astonishment? Disgust? Something else.

"I have another question," Jeanie announced. "About the climbing tree."

This time Roberta let out a tormented little moan.

"Listen.... My dad... won't talk about it." Roberta's voice sounded shaky.

Jeanie cut in impatiently. "I just want to know what you did with my stuff."

This statement silenced the table.

"What stuff, J?" Mrs. Shade finally asked.

"I kept some stuff inside the climbing tree and I want it back."

Mrs. Shade's eyebrows shot up. "You kept things inside of it? Where?"

"In the hole."

"There was a hole in the tree?"

"Yes there was a hole, and I dropped a little sack on a string inside it, a sack with my stuff, and I want it back."

Mrs. Shade's voice had more than its usual sharpness. "Do you mean the tree was hollow?"

"I *just said* I kept my stuff inside a hole in the tree," Jeanie snapped. Then silence settled back over the table.

The tree was hollow. Laurel's mother, clearly, found that very significant. Why? Laurel needed to think....

Then Jeanie let out a dramatic gasp. "*Pause the conversation!* My TV is being interrupted by a special bulletin!"

Something truly important was happening right now, something about the climbing tree—this was no time for Jeanie's television. "Shush, Jeanie," Laurel exclaimed. "You can be such an *infant* sometimes!"

"Well, then you're a fetus."

"A fetus," Laurel repeated. "A *fetus.* How can you even know what that means? You're only seven years old!"

"Seven *earth* years," Jeanie said.

A machine-gun-like burst of laughter sounded out. Laurel felt a sudden dampness. A fine spray of milk coated her neck and upper arm.

It had come from Computer Dave. The laugh had been his, erupting through a mouthful of milk. Laurel looked over at him, startled, and then quickly looked away. She did not want to see his dignity shredded like this. And she did not want that machine-gun laugh to belong to him. It left her feeling empty and somehow excluded.

Mrs. Shade had chosen to politely ignore the milk eruption. "You're in rare form tonight, Jeanie," was all she said.

"At least *I* don't have milk dripping out of my nose," Jeanie said. She handed Computer Dave a thick stack of napkins, then passed some to Laurel.

Marcus Vaughn and his family came into the restaurant just then. "Hello, Nancy," Mrs. Shade greeted his mother. Mrs. Vaughn smiled coldly. The Vaughn kids looked away.

Mrs. Shade frowned. "Time to go," she said, and stood up.

They got home very late for a school night. Dr. Shade was there, grumbling about coming home to an empty house. Then everyone went to bed and things got quiet. Except inside Laurel's head.

The climbing tree... hollow... why had the Holyfields' dad cut it down? How had he even cut it down, for that matter? He couldn't have done it all by himself, Laurel realized for the first time.... *Roberta*... so alone... why had she lost interest in the search for her brother? *Computer Dave—the real David Holyfield*... why oh why *oh why* couldn't Laurel get control of this painful tangle of feelings? *The computer*... if it did have a conflict among the interrupts, Laurel thought suddenly, why couldn't someone—someone like Mr. Schmitt—simply figure out which components used the same interrupts? Then she'd know which things might have gotten confused! She could probably find the switched files....

With these thoughts circling in her head like horses on a merry-go-round, Laurel slipped into a turbulent sleep.

Sometime later—how long?—Laurel woke suddenly. She thought a sound had woken her. A raspy, empty sound.

Laurel made herself as still as possible, her breathing shallow, sheets unmoving. She lay like that for minutes. No sound.

She settled back, started drifting to sleep, when there it was again—a raspy noise that raised goose bumps on her scalp.

The streetlight cast dark gray shadows of tree limbs onto the wall over Jeanie's bed, and they thrashed silently. And then *something on that wall moved.*

Something was moving on the wall—not a shadow but something three-dimensional. Some grotesque shape was moving up near the ceiling. It seemed to be *squeezing itself out of the wall* and *oozing down it* silently—and now oozing onto Jeanie's bed. Laurel gasped.

She snapped on the light.

Nightshade, startled in the act of shaking himself off, stared at Laurel from Jeanie's bed. His eyes glowed like small lanterns. On the wall high above him, the metal grate that covered the air vent swung loosely, like a pet door.

The Shades were all gathered around Jeanie's bed. Dr. Shade was chuckling. "I guess Nightshade's gotten to know the whole heating system. At least a couple of the grates are loose enough that he can push them open with his paw. The one in our bedroom and the one in yours. Once he gets inside the duct, he can travel through the house. He's got his own transportation network. A little dusty, though."

"Just look at him—I never saw him so dirty," Mrs. Shade said. "Ah, now he's cleaning himself."

All eyes turned to Nightshade, who was now a frenzied, fur-licking pretzel.

"He certainly is," Dr. Shade said dryly. "I've never seen such a cleaning. That cat is cleaning himself to beat the band."

" 'To beat the band'—what band?" Laurel asked.

"It's an expression. It means you're doing whatever you're doing in a really big way. Come to think of it, I'm not sure what a band has to do with anything."

"I know, I know!" Jeanie cried shrilly. " 'To beat the band.' It means you're doing whatever you're doing with so much… *oomph* that you could drown out the band's music. And you know how I know? Because they have the *exact same expression in Turbish!*"

And so ended the mystery of Nightshade.

It all made sense. Case closed. Laurel even observed to herself that it wasn't too surprising Nightshade ended up on Jeanie's bed so much, since it was right under the vent.

And yet there was no denying it, she felt oddly deflated.

Why on earth should Laurel be feeling let down? What had she expected?

She'd just thought it was something more… something more.

chapter 19

In the kitchen the next morning her mother keeps giving Laurel a sappy, irritating look. Then she starts massaging Laurel's back. "Think you'll be okay at school today?"

Laurel tenses her back muscles and pulls away. She has a headache and her eyes are sore. Her stomach feels as if some scared little creature is living in it, like a chipmunk or maybe a squirrel.

She's hardly slept at all. First getting home late from Lilacs, then the whole Nightshade thing. After that she just tossed. And now it's time to go to school. As an outcast.

"I don't want to go to school today," she says. "I hate school."

"Honey, don't say that. Would you like me to pick you up today?" Her mother just isn't acting like herself. She's talking in a voice designed for babies, cooing, practically.

Laurel feels a small explosion inside.

"I DON'T WANT TO GO TO SCHOOL! Didn't you hear me? I don't even want to live here! I HATE CHEST-NUT KNOLL, don't you understand?"

Never in her life has Laurel talked like this. She's the considerate one, the controlled one. Wow, is that really *her* voice? Its raging sound is intoxicating.

Now her mother is cooing again. "I don't want to hear you talk that way, honey." This comment fuels Laurel's rage.

"I *do not understand* what you and Dad want from me! You're always saying you want me to think for myself, and now when I criticize this horrible place, you tell me not to talk that way. You don't know how everyone's treating Roberta and her brother—they're hating them and being horrible and—*nobody even knows anything!*"

Mrs. Shade doesn't answer for a long time. *She knows I'm right,* Laurel thinks.

And her mother's first words are confirming. "Laurel, you know I'm proud of you. You know that, right?" Mrs. Shade starts to reach for Laurel's hand, then seems to change her mind. *She's a little bit afraid of me right now,* Laurel realizes.

When Mrs. Shade begins again, she is obviously choosing her words with care. "I may know more than you think, honey. I know that people are way too quick to judge. We're all so darn quick to judge. It seems like we're made that way. It's like instinct or something. Maybe that's how we escaped from the saber-toothed tiger, back when we lived in caves. We made a snap judgment and bolted. And now there aren't any more saber-toothed tigers but we still make those snap judgments anyway. And it can be very unfair."

"And totally stupid! And horrible!"

"Yes. But anyway. You know something? The people in Chestnut Knoll aren't any worse than anyplace else. At least people here care about things. They care about their community. And yes, they're quick to judge, but…"

"But *what?* BUT WHAT? It's okay to ruin these kids' lives?" Laurel's voice is still raging.

Her mother starts to say something, then stops herself. She sighs. "Just keep on keeping your head. And I love you. That's all."

Laurel pulls away and runs out of the house. She's headed for the Holyfields'.

The fact is, she doesn't *want* to keep her head. Why can't her mother just say, you poor baby, they *are* all horrible and you're right to hate them?

But as Laurel pounds down the trail, other parts of what her mother said are seeping in. Quick to judge. That's it, all right. Everyone is so unbelievably quick to judge. Maybe we can't help it, but... No. That can't be right.

Laurel arrived breathless at the Holyfields'. Roberta answered the door. Her father wasn't home—of course—and Computer Dave had gone in early to finish some project.

Roberta looked small and alone and anxious. Looking at her, Laurel felt her rage drain away.

"Hey, listen. I have a new idea about finding your brother in the computer," she said, forcing a brisk tone into her voice.

Roberta just looked at her.

All at once, Laurel felt foolish. The idea of a human brain lost in a computer suddenly seemed totally preposterous.

Heat surged into her face. "Just forget it. I'm an idiot."

Roberta was immediately horrified. "No you're not! I'm really sorry. I'm kind of, like, distracted, I guess. Tell me again. I promise I'll listen this time. Please tell me your idea."

"It's nothing. It's stupid," Laurel responded, but Roberta continued to coax. Finally Laurel gave in and described her idea.

She proposed to have Mr. Schmitt examine the computer David had used. Laurel explained about the interrupt. She thought Mr. Schmitt would be able to tell whether the interrupt codes had been set up in a way that created a conflict. "I bet Mr. Schmitt can get to the bottom of it. But he's got to see the computer. Can we take it to school? We don't need the monitor or keyboard or anything, just the box with the CPU. It's not all that heavy by itself. Your dad's not here now, right? We can bring it back after school today and he'll never even know it was gone."

Roberta agreed. But that anxious look had come back to her face.

The box was, in fact, very heavy. They began walking slowly, unsteadily, holding the computer in quivering arms, cords dragging behind.

"This thing is heavy!" Roberta gasped. They walked for an eternity. It was hard to keep a grip on the metal sides of the computer.

"*Lug* is a good word, don't you think?" Roberta said at one point. And a few steps later: "*Trudge,* too. *Trudge* is another good word."

"I don't think we can possibly get this all the way to school," Roberta said when they had stopped to rest for the fifth or sixth time. "My arms are burning. They're jelly. They're burning jelly."

"Oh, Roberta, we have to!"

"I just can't, Laurel. My arms are shaking so much I'm afraid I'll drop it."

Laurel glanced back to gauge their progress. Incredibly, they had gone less than half a block.

And what on earth? There was Jeanie! She was frantically waving her arms. "Wait right there, you two! I'm going to get the CTD!" she shouted. Jeanie must have followed her to the Holyfields', Laurel realized.

Now Jeanie was shouting again. "I'll be back in a couple of minutes with the CTD!"

Laurel and Roberta looked at each other, mystified. But Laurel actually didn't mind an excuse to flop down. She massaged her arm muscles. They already looked bigger.

A few minutes later Jeanie was back. "Hold on! I've got the CTD!" She was scuttling toward them, shoulders hunched, pushing a plastic car.

It was a Little Tikes car, yellow on top, red on the bottom, and it steered crazily. As it got closer, Laurel saw that it was covered in cobwebs. She had not seen it in years, not since Jeanie was a toddler.

"Look, it's perfect, and it was right in the garage," Jeanie said breathlessly. "The CTD." As Laurel and Roberta exchanged puzzled looks, Jeanie cried, "The Computer Transport Device!"

If both of its doors were left open, like red plastic wings, the Little Tikes car could just hold the computer. The car had a tendency to turn in circles. But once they worked out a system, one girl guiding each side and one pushing from the rear, the trip was smooth. Even the street curbs were manageable. They all had sloping concrete sections for wheelchairs.

As they pushed, Roberta looked back at Jeanie in the rear position. "You really saved us, Jeanie! How did you know we needed help?"

"Oh, you know, there was an emergency bulletin on my television screen. It was during *The Skunky and Splat Show.*"

"During... *what?*" asked Roberta.

"*Skunky and Splat!* Oh, Laurel, did I tell you? They figured out how to make these cool sounds no one ever discovered before...."

But thankfully, they were now at the school. They pushed the Little Tikes car over near the bike rack. Laurel ran in and got Mr. Schmitt, who carried the computer inside. He actually made it look easy.

In Laurel's classroom that morning the bad dream of yesterday continued. No one acknowledged her. Her old classroom friendships seemed increasingly unreal in her memory, like the trip to that island in the Caribbean the Shades had taken one winter. The only thing to look forward to was computer class.

But Mr. Schmitt wasn't quite himself in class that day. He could not stop talking, for one thing. As he talked, he slipped into lecture mode, and then into something more: something more like a sermon, noble and lofty. He was talking about the promise of a computerized world.

His big message was that everything in the world had been united by digitization. Every conceivable type of information could now be digitized: typed or scanned or somehow coded into a computer, hooked up to the Internet, and thus made available to the whole universe. And not just written information—everything. Sounds, movement, even smells.

Science, too! The Human Genome Project, the scientific effort to map the entire human DNA sequence, had already posted its results on the Internet. And government! Official documents of every kind were rapidly migrating to the Web. In this respect, Mr. Schmitt said, Chestnut Knoll's government was ahead of most. The town's property records had been computerized for some time, and had recently been made accessible to the general public on the Internet.

Everything was becoming knowable to everyone at the click of a button.

Mr. Schmitt's eyes were closed. He might have been reciting poetry. "Computers have allowed us to conquer two things. The first one, the one I just talked about, is *space*. Distance has totally collapsed. With the Internet, for all practical purposes, the whole world now occupies a single point in space."

Mr. Schmitt took a deep breath. "But that's just the beginning. Let me tell you about the second step. Let me tell you about conquering *time*."

He glanced briefly at Laurel, then continued. "In many ways the human brain operates in a binary fashion. So does a computer. And both also operate by means of electronic impulses. So because of the binary, electronic basis of human thought—*human thought*—there is no reason why at some future point we shouldn't be able to download digitized information directly to our brains. And vice versa. The contents of our brains can be uploaded, if you will. Transmitted directly into a computer and stored there. With a little refining of current MRI and scanning technology, we'll be able to map the human brain and then preserve it electronically.

"Then our individual brains can merge in one huge super-computer. We're talking about perfect unity. Total knowledge. *Truly conquering time.* Because when the contents of our brain can be transferred to a computer file, we will no longer be dependent on these bodies, these fragile bodies of ours that get sick and die. Our thoughts will be able to live forever, to continue developing, to merge with the thoughts of others...."

It was quite a vision. The students seemed stunned. They sat frozen in their seats. Several mouths hung open.

Finally a stage whisper rose from the back of the room: "He's mental!"

But Laurel had been transported to another world. She looked over at Computer Dave. *Mr. Schmitt's future is already here,* she thought.

When the bell rang for her lunch period, Laurel rushed up the stairs, back to the computer lab. Mr. Schmitt, coat on, was locking the door. When he saw Laurel, his face grew troubled.

"I'm late for a meeting right now," he told her. "But I'm afraid I have some bad news about your computer. I haven't finished looking at it yet, but the hard drive is dying. I think it's corrupting a lot of the files. From what I can tell so far, there's one huge file that's been totally destroyed. Maybe that's why you weren't finding that really big file you were looking for. I think it's in smithereens all over the hard drive."

One huge file had been blown to smithereens. It was splattered all over the place.

Laurel felt ill. "Is there any way to fix it?"

Mr. Schmitt looked discouraged. "Listen, stop by after school today and we can talk about whether there's some kind of backup. Or maybe I can put my hands on some disk-repair utility that can fix it. I've got to be honest with you, though. It's a real mess."

Laurel moved down the steps, stunned. She paused uncertainly in the main corridor of the school. She didn't know what to do with herself. Roberta's class wouldn't be on the playground for another half hour. Laurel wasn't supposed to leave the building without an adult. And no power on earth was getting her near the lunchroom today.

She watched a couple of fifth-grade girls and a mom, giggling and presenting a cupcake to the secretary in the main office. They were going out to lunch. It must be someone's birthday.

Laurel moved forward. She edged just close enough to blend with the birthday group without getting them suspicious. She glided along just behind the trio, outside and down the stairs.

No one stopped her. It was weirdly thrilling.

When she reached the sidewalk, she began taking huge, hard steps, walking in a direction she rarely went. The images that ran through her mind were violent ones, pictures of gooey splattered things: Smashed pumpkins. Roadkill. Thrown pies. She tramped on; she had a half hour to fill with her steps. Good Lord, what was she going to say to Roberta about her brother?

She had no idea of the time. In her morning rage, she had forgotten her watch. When she looked around, she was in an unfamiliar neighborhood. Maybe she had walked too far. Now she really had no idea of the time.

She came to a store, which looked out of place at the end of a row of houses. Nickelby's, the store was called. Laurel went inside. She looked around for a clock but didn't see one. She walked over to a man standing behind the counter reading from a clipboard. He looked up. His dark eyes were large and liquid and warm-looking.

"Did you want to buy something?"

Laurel hesitated. "I just need to know what time it is. Do you have a watch?"

The man just looked back at his clipboard without bothering to answer.

The rage that Laurel had discovered in herself that morning started to nudge its way up again. "Excuse me," she said loudly. "Could you please tell me what time it is?"

The man still didn't answer; he barely glanced at her. But now she saw it—just behind the liquidness of his eyes was a hardness, almost a cruelty. Why hadn't she seen it before?

"How can you run a store without some kind of clock?" Now the full-blown rage was back in her voice. *"And how can you not even answer me?"*

She left, slamming the door behind her.

Laurel headed back toward school, heart racing. She thought again of David Holyfield, the real David Holyfield, who might be in unrecoverable fragments all over the computer hard drive.

She thought of Roberta, all by herself on the playground.

And she thought about that evil Nickelby's man. Yes, evil, *purely evil,* even though he'd looked like someone from a book of saints. How dare he have those warm, liquid eyes? The world *should not allow* such evil people.

Oh man, I'm in a state, she said to herself. That's what her grandmother would call it.

Then all at once she thought of Cleve. That uninviting stout red face of his. He'd do anything for anyone.

The idea slowed her down. Then it brought her to a standstill.

Wonderful Cleve. His face had come so strangely into her mind, so suddenly. *"Lovely Laurel of the Shade variety,"* she could hear him saying. And *"Pleased to meet you, Madame X."*

Oh Cleve! she thought with fervor. *You and your kind, kind heart.*

Now something peculiar was happening. Her rage almost seemed to be vaporizing—changing into an oddly joyous energy. She felt tingly and helium-light. Okay, she said to herself. The world did allow that evil Nickelby's man. But there were Cleves out there, too.

She began to move again. Then faster, and then faster.

Rushing now, surging along, her feet barely skimming the ground.

Now in sight of school. Now onto the blacktop.

She spotted Roberta, far off, sitting on the same wall as yesterday.

They were all there, the same staring cliques, the clusters. The card traders, the boxballers, the gymnasts, the gossips. But there would be no molasses walk today. Today she would soar across the playground. She was Supergirl. She could fly.

"Wait, Laurel! Laurel Shade!"

Laurel stopped. She turned around.

Felicity Osterman was hurrying after her. "Wait, Laurel! You are like breaking the speed limit! Where are you going?"

For a moment Laurel couldn't answer. She was out of breath, to her great surprise, and just stood there gasping, hands on her sides.

"Laurel, are you okay and everything? I kept wanting to talk to you all day yesterday but you were so, like… unapproachable."

Laurel was astonished.

"So where are you going, Laurel?"

Now Laurel had her breath back. "I'm going to sit with that girl on the wall over there. Roberta Holyfield."

"I'm coming, too," Felicity said. She then executed a cartwheel so flawless it became impossible to disagree.

They headed toward Roberta, Felicity skipping, Laurel thinking, *I love you, Felicity.*

★ ★ ★

Roberta looked up from the low stone wall. First she looked at Laurel, then at Felicity. And one more time: first Laurel, then Felicity. Then Roberta's face went into freeze-frame right between the two of them. Her eyes were fixed on some spot in the middle and just above their shoulders.

A change came over Roberta's face that was unforgettable. It was a slow-motion smile that gradually turned her cheeks into carved globes and showed her perfect teeth.

Laurel watched Roberta's face transform, astonished. Then she turned around. She was looking into another huge smile, another set of carved-globe cheeks, and more perfect teeth. It was Aubrey Madison.

chapter 20

Aubrey Madison on the playground—talk about strange! Aubrey is supposed to arrive in some exotic car just as the bell rings. Yet here she is, all right, and she's glowing like a sunrise. Roberta is on one side of her and Laurel on the other. Felicity cavorts in front of them.

The playground hums with astonishment. Aubrey Madison! On the Tuckerman playground!

She is talking to Roberta about modeling. "You've got a good look. A little exotic or something. Even the glasses are cute!"

Roberta just arches her eyebrows.

Aubrey prods her. "So how does that sound to you?"

"Ridiculous," says Roberta.

Aubrey laughs, a husky laugh, very cool-sounding. Her black hair puffs out around her face. *She belongs in the middle of an admiring crowd,* Laurel thinks. *She's the most stunning girl in Westchester.*

In the distance a loose ring of Tuckerman students has formed. All eyes are on Aubrey.

It's not easy talking to Aubrey as if she's a regular kid. First of all, she's gorgeous, of course. But then there's also the pull of her personality. Up close like this, Laurel is really feeling it for the first time. It's like some natural force, like gravity or magnetism.

Hey, maybe—and this idea now strikes Laurel like a brick on the head—maybe Aubrey's attractiveness isn't really all that much about how she looks. Maybe it's that… *stuff* she radiates. That warmth, that confidence, that serenity.

The entire playground is vibrating with excitement over Aubrey.

Laurel watches Aubrey beaming at Roberta. Just then Aubrey looks over at Laurel and sends her one of those blazing smiles.

Can there be such a thing in this world as a purely good person? Maybe that's what Aubrey is. Why else, Laurel wonders, should she do this amazing thing? From the great heights she had somehow sensed their need, and like a kind of angel had come down to help.

Aubrey does live on the heights—that's for certain. She seems to have it all. But who can really say what's in her heart? Maybe Aubrey—forever above, forever apart—feels a kinship with outsiders.

Finally Felicity comes to rest. "You being on the playground feels so weird, Aubrey. I feel like I should be asking for your autograph or something."

"This girl," says Aubrey firmly, "has done too many cartwheels."

Felicity lets out a goofy cackle. Then they all start quaking with laughter.

Giddiness has totally taken them over. The rest of the Tuckerman students gape.

All the way home with Roberta, Laurel's feet seemed to want to tap-dance. What *was* that song her heels were clicking out? "The Bear Went over the Mountain," she decided. An elated feeling was pushing up inside like carbonated bubbles. "Things are *so much better,*" she exulted.

But Roberta was chewing her lip. "To tell you the truth, I'll be happy if I can just get through the evening. You know that

Conservation Board meeting is tonight. And my father—so typi-
cal!" She sputtered, suddenly, in a way that sounded like someone
else. "He refuses to even go."

Guilt and regret came piling down on Laurel. How could she
have been so thoughtless? Things might look better for her, but
Roberta's situation was still pretty miserable. There was still the
problem of her brother: *one huge file… in smithereens….* And there
was still the whole huge climbing-tree mess.

"Oh man. Why *on earth* would your father do it? I mean, the
tree?" The question spilled out before Laurel even thought.

Roberta continued to chew on her lip. "There are a lot of
things I can't talk to my dad about," she finally said quietly. "Like
the tree. I've pushed as far as I can. And he's just not going to do
anything to help himself. And that meeting is *tonight*." She finished
with a sort of moan.

This poor kid, Laurel thought. *Okay, Supergirl, do something.*

"Roberta, listen. You know this tree thing isn't just your dad's
business, it has a huge effect on you and your brother, too. If your
dad isn't going to do anything, then you and I will have to."

"Like what? What can we do?"

"I started thinking," Laurel said. "He couldn't have cut the tree
down by himself. He must have hired somebody. And whoever
cut down that tree would know something. We should talk to that
person."

"I know he hired someone, but I don't know who."

"We'll figure it out," Laurel said. *I am* really *determined,* she
thought.

Inside the Holyfields' house, Roberta was jumpy as a rabbit. She
had no idea when her father was coming home. He could return
any second.

Laurel figured that if Roberta's father had arranged for

someone to do tree work, he had probably kept the phone number tucked away somewhere. The Shades kept fat stacks of business cards from people like painters and plumbers. She told Roberta that they should check in the places where her father might keep those kinds of papers.

Roberta took her to Mr. Holyfield's office. It turned out to be in the basement of the house.

The two of them peered into the office from the doorway. It was a small white room with low ceiling tiles, bright fluorescent lighting, and a slightly musty odor. It had one vine-covered window near the top of one of the walls. The room contained a white filing cabinet, a computer equipment stand, and a large, spotless desk, empty except for computer and telephone. It was all as white and orderly and bright as an operating room. There didn't seem to be any paper anywhere.

"Where do you think he'd keep his address book?" Laurel hurried over to the desk and began opening drawers, quickly and nervously. "Doesn't your dad use any paper at all?"

"He's very computerized," Roberta said. "Log on, quick, see what you can find on the computer. The password is *intrepid.*"

Then a loud thumping noise came from upstairs.

Roberta's terrified gaze locked with Laurel's. "I'm going to check upstairs," Roberta breathed. "Just hurry!"

Laurel turned on the computer, which began crunching and gurgling softly. While she waited for it to boot up, her foot tapped frantically. It was taking forever.

When the monitor finally displayed the opening desktop icons, Laurel hunted for an icon that looked like an address book. No luck. So she clicked on a START button that displayed a list of the computer's contents.

Up came the list, but which option did she want? Would a computerized phone book be a Program? An Accessory? A

Document? Might it be under Office? Or Favorites? What if she needed to know some other password?

By then Roberta had returned. She leaned far into the room without actually stepping over the threshold. "No, no, no, go back to the icons, that desktop part," she coached anxiously. "Click on that yellow one! That little yellow icon in the bottom row!"

"You mean this thing that looks like a taxicab?"

"Yes, yes, hurry up, that one! It's supposed to look like a telephone. I think that's where the phone numbers are."

Roberta was right. A double-click on the yellow icon took Laurel into some kind of phone directory. TYPE IN LAST NAME OR FIRST FEW LETTERS, the top of the screen commanded her. ALL ENTRIES BEGINNING WITH THOSE LETTERS WILL BE DISPLAYED.

Laurel gritted her teeth and growled softly. She didn't know the last name, did she? That was the problem. In desperation, she simply typed in "tree."

While she waited for the search results, a particularly loud thump from the upstairs made her pop up out of the chair.

"It's the washing machine—it's banging," Roberta whispered. "Sorry, I should have told you. But hurry, okay? I mean, someone just put a load of laundry in, so my dad might walk in any second."

Finally the screen flashed the search results. TREE WORK: CONTI LANDSCAPING AND TREE WORK. "Yes!" Laurel hissed, triumphant. "Conti Landscaping!"

"Have you heard of him?" Roberta asked.

Laurel was practically dancing. "Have I heard of him? I *know* him!"

Mr. Conti did yard work for the Shades and many of their friends. His red baseball cap and red truck, with CONTI LAND-SCAPING AND TREE WORK painted on the side, were familiar sights in the neighborhood. Surely he would remember about the climbing tree. Wouldn't he?

Just then another sound came from upstairs. Was it a door being slammed? Laurel bolted out of the office and clutched at Roberta, who pulled her toward a basement door.

"You'd better go out this way." Roberta looked panicked.

In spite of Laurel's hammering heart, the determined feeling was still with her. "Don't worry, Roberta," she said. "I'll call Mr. Conti. I'll take care of everything, I promise."

She rushed out the basement door and then CRACK— buzzing, sizzling pain.

She had banged her funny bone on the doorjamb, hard, and the pain was electrifying. It was turning the world to gold and black. She was no longer sure if she was standing or floating.

With an enormous effort, Laurel willed herself to stay silent and keep moving. She rushed along, clutching the injured elbow, muttering to herself to keep from yelling. *Holy smoke, holy moly,* she said through her teeth. *Holy Toledo, holy cow, holy Christmas...*

Halfway home, she finally wailed out loud. "Holy *crap!* The *computer.*" She had just remembered that they had left the Holyfields' computer at school, and now the building was closed. They'd left the Little Tikes car, too.

And even worse—she had forgotten to turn off Mr. Holyfield's computer. It was still running in his basement office. Was it too late to call Roberta and warn her?

But the top priority was to get in touch with Mr. Conti before the meeting that night. After all, she had promised Roberta she would take care of everything.

The next two hours passed in a blur.

When Laurel called Mr. Conti's number, it turned out to be the number of his pager. She had to wait and wait for him to call back.

But Mr. Conti finally did return her call. And he had lots to say about the climbing tree.

chapter 21

Jeanie shudders. "I think I maybe *hate* this channel. That chairman guy looks so *nasty*." And for once all the Shades agree.

They are gathered in front of the television. The Conservation Board meeting is being broadcast on the local cable channel and has just begun.

For Laurel, the suspense is huge. Every muscle twitches. Her teeth are practically chattering. Now she knows what should happen. Or, at least, she knows what she believes should happen. But will it?

Chairman Wagner wore glasses low on his nose. Their lenses weren't much bigger than Scrabble tiles. He squinted around the room irritably.

"I see we have more than our usual number of spectators tonight." The chairman's words were followed by a metallic squeal, and his voice, over the squealing, turned snappish. "Can someone please adjust this microphone?"

When the long microphone squeal finally ended, he spoke

again. "Copies of the agenda are being handed out." He sent a withering look over the Scrabble-tile glasses to one of the spectators. "You'll get one, sir, you really will."

An anxious-looking woman with a bright blue blouse leaned over Chairman Wagner's shoulder and whispered something.

The chairman cringed. "What is it now, *Ms.* Bauer?" He pronounced the "Ms." with an exaggerated buzzing sound, like "Mzzzzzz."

Once again she whispered, and then the chairman turned back to the microphone. "My staff director tells me that many of you in the audience are interested in the tree business, so the board is moving that up to item number one. Now where's that petition?"

He removed a paper from Ms. Bauer's nervous fingers. "A petition was presented asking this board to take action in the matter of a tree cut down on the Chestnut Knoll Nature Trail. Is that the new survey? Yes, that's it."

After a moment the TV camera zeroed in on a chart. It showed a thick jagged line that seemed to connect several puzzle pieces. The bottom of the chart read BOUNDARY—CHESTNUT KNOLL NATURE TRAIL.

Laurel jumped up off her cushion. She moved close to the TV for a better look.

Off camera, the chairman's voice went on. "This is a very current survey of the Chestnut Knoll Nature Trail. We commissioned it when we received the petition, and it was completed just a couple days ago."

The chairman's voice got louder. "Take a good look. As you can see, the boundary of the nature trail is not very regular. Look at this piece here. It kind of cuts into the trail like a little triangle. That's the old Brenningmeyer lot, the land that's now owned by... let's see. A Mr. Holyfield."

After some rustling of papers, the chairman's voice continued.

"My staff did a little research. Apparently this Brenningmeyer, the original owner of that lot, was quite a guy. He moved to Chestnut Knoll in the 1920s. He set up a free school, teaching English to immigrants…. Before that, he'd been a missionary in China.

"Now, when the nature trail was established in the 1930s, the town of Chestnut Knoll took over a fair-sized strip of land for the trail. But they didn't want to disrupt the property holdings too much. And the Brenningmeyer lot was small to begin with, so they kind of carved the bottom of it out from the trail, that little piece of pie there."

All this time the camera had stayed focused on the chart. Now a pointer appeared and touched several circles on the chart. The circles were all drawn directly on top of the Holyfield lot's property line.

"These circles show where trees are located. Smack on the property line. Brenningmeyer probably planted them there to mark the boundary. Could be trees he brought back from China. Planted halfway on his land, halfway off."

Laurel sucked in her breath—this was not what she'd expected. Had she made some incredibly stupid mistake? Her heart seemed to be creeping up toward her throat.

As the pointer lingered over one of the circles, the chairman's voice grew sharper. "Now, here's the issue. It's really a legal issue, so the staff attorney will need to do some research on it. This here, that's the trunk of the old cork tree. As you can see, it straddles the property line. So who owns the tree? The owner of the lot? Or the town? And if the town owns even a small part of a tree, doesn't that make it improper for the private landowner to take it down? Would a responsible person cut down a tree that he didn't entirely own?"

The audience tittered. The chairman glared over the Scrabble tiles.

Laurel's whole body had clenched. Something was going

wrong. And she'd promised Roberta she'd take care of everything! Poor Roberta—was she watching right now? Was her face crumbling?

Laurel began nibbling at the skin around her fingernails.

Then a man's broad back moved in front of the camera. The man was apparently saying something to the chairman, who squinted and snapped.

"Well, I suppose so. But for God's sake, come up and use a microphone so I don't have to repeat every word."

Jeanie let out a squeal. "It's Mr. Conti! Look look look, it's Mr. Conti!"

"No it isn't," said their mother. "Wait a minute, yes it is! My goodness, it's Mr. Conti without his baseball cap. I can't imagine what he has to say."

But Laurel could. She could imagine every word.

Mr. Conti bent his head down and introduced himself, and the microphone snarled back at him.

"I'd like to add my two cents now, if I can," he said after putting some distance between himself and the microphone. "Mr. Holyfield called me about some yard work back two, three months ago. Just moved here. You know, that little house was empty for a long time, and the yard looked pretty bad. So me and Holyfield, we're looking around and talking about what needs doing, you know, the tree work, some drainage problems, and so forth. So while we're talking, I point to the tree and says, you should call the town, that tree's getting to be a real hazard.

"He says, I been wondering about that tree. What makes you say it's in such bad shape? See, this Holyfield guy doesn't really know trees. He says, maybe it's supposed to look like that.

"I says, no way. Just look at the branches, see how they're so twisty? Especially up top. Twisted like corkscrews, some of them. That's a virus that does that, a tree virus. Plus, I can see the thing's hollow. Big hole just above a major branch. Squirrels running in and out. I says, thing could come down next big wind. And haven't you seen how the kids like to climb that tree? It's dangerous. And then Holyfield says, that's my tree, not the town's. He says, the whole thing's on my property."

The audience rumbled.

Mr. Conti waited for the noise to subside. Then he continued. "Guy says, since it's on my property and you're saying it's dangerous, I guess I have the liability. So go ahead. Take it down. And I says, fine. Bottom line is, no matter whose property, that tree had to come down. It was rotted away. Just go look at the trunk of it now. The wood's all dark, instead of light like it should be. It wasn't safe anymore, what with the kids climbing on it all the time."

The background rumble again swelled up, and Mr. Conti paused again.

"Anyway, today someone calls me. A gal from the neighborhood."

Laurel's heart was now wedged in her throat. She gnawed ferociously at her fingertips.

"This gal wants to know what's the story with the tree. And I told her what happened. And how Holyfield said the tree was on *his* land. So she says to me, don't I think I ought to go to the Conservation Board meeting?"

Mr. Conti chuckled. "And she says she thinks the town property records are on the Internet—she learned it in computer science class, if you can believe it. She says she's going to do some research, see if she can find the records on the Web. Didn't she get in touch with you folks?"

The chairman looked dour. "I don't believe so."

For a while Mr. Conti didn't say anything. Then he shifted his wide shoulders uneasily.

"No offense or anything. But when was the last time you checked your e-mail?"

Ms. Bauer, looking stricken, jumped up. She held another whispered conference with the chairman. Then she hurried away.

The chairman sighed into the microphone. "Let's take a ten-minute break, everyone."

In the pause that followed, the first thing Laurel did was gulp down a giant glass of water. She was trying to clear a pathway in her throat.

"I wonder where that poor Miss Bauer scurried off to," Mrs. Shade said.

"Don't you mean *Mzzzzz*. Bauer? I guess she's checking their e-mail." Dr. Shade sounded amused. "I wouldn't want to be in that woman's shoes for all the tea in China. But you know what I want to know—which 'gal' had the presence of mind to call Mr. Conti?"

Before anyone could answer, Mrs. Shade gasped. "My God, Laurel! *What on earth have you done to your hands?*"

Laurel looked down. All that nervous gnawing had made her fingers bleed.

When the ten-minute break ended, the camera focused on two black-and-white sheets of paper that someone had taped on top of the nature trail chart.

"Well, guess what was waiting for us?" the chairman's voice said off camera. "Someone did send us an e-mail. Don't know the person's name, just the screen name. Shadybug 88."

Mrs. Shade jerked as if struck by lightning. She leaned toward Laurel, intent. *"Shadybug 88!"* she hissed.

Chairman Wagner continued. "Anyway, this e-mail correspondent pointed us to the land records that the town has posted on the Internet. So we went to that Web site and printed out some things. I know they're hard to make out, especially on television, and I apologize."

The camera zoomed in on the chairman's finger pointing to the papers. "So these are from the official property records, the ones on file with the town. These are the plats from a survey done in 1933, when the nature trail was established. And I have to emphasize something—in the audience you probably can't see this very clearly. *This* survey, this older survey, shows the old cork tree *totally inside the boundaries* of this lot—you know, the lot that is now owned by Mr. Holyfield.

"After that, obviously, the tree grew, and spilled over the property line—as we saw before, on that new survey. But this survey *here,* this 1933 one, is the official one. If you're searching for property records on the Internet, this is what you find. That may be what Mr. Holyfield did."

The camera returned to the chairman. "I must say it's annoying we haven't heard from him. He did get a notice about this meeting, didn't he?" He sent a look in Ms. Bauer's direction. "And for future reference, in a case like this, I suggest my staff look at the official property records sooner rather than later."

Chairman Wagner paused. He made an adjustment to his cuff. "We'll need to get the attorney's opinion. But at this point *I'm* certainly sympathetic to a landowner who relies on the official plats. I mean, it's fine for us to pay for a new survey that shows trees have grown and spilled over onto town property, but I don't know that regular people can be expected to do that whenever they have tree work done."

The background rumbling became a roar. One sound rose over the general commotion. A woman, apparently a board member, was speaking. But on television her actual words could not be heard— just the sound of her voice, like the humming of a huge insect.

The chairman listened, looking cranky. "Let me repeat what Mrs. Loft is saying. She is asking whether there is any ordinance that would forbid people from *affecting* town property like the nature trail—from having an impact on town property—even if the tree they remove or whatever isn't actually *on* town property."

The voice buzzed once more.

The chairman sniffed. "Or is only partly on town property. Well, you understand that this is turning into a very different issue from the one presented by the petition. Do I have a motion to place this item on the agenda for the next meeting and arrange for the appropriate legal work?"

A long mumble followed.

"Do I have a second?" the chairman asked, and then, after a much shorter responding mumble: "Would you be so kind as to take care of this? *Ms.* Bauer?"

For a long time after the television was clicked off, the Shades sat staring at its empty screen. Nightshade climbed on top of the television and settled there, his paws tucked under him. He looked like a hen warming its eggs.

"So what happens next?" Laurel finally asked.

No one said anything for a while. Then her mother spoke. "Well, you heard that one woman on the board say maybe it's against the law to do something that has an impact on the trail, even if the thing you do is mostly on your own property. So they're going to talk about it at their next meeting."

"But anyway," Dr. Shade cut in, "now everyone knows that the Holyfields had good reason to think the tree was on their land. And everyone heard Mr. Conti say the tree had a virus. It'll be really hard to keep making an issue about this."

"So now," said Jeanie, "the question becomes: what did *Mr. Conti* do with my stuff?"

"Oh, Jeanie, please," said Mrs. Shade. "But isn't it just so strange? How we didn't hear any of this till now? Why didn't that Holyfield man tell anyone?"

"Nobody bothered to ask," said Dr. Shade. "And he was new in town. He didn't know anything."

"Why didn't he at least show up at the meeting?"

"That would have been a lot more satisfying, wouldn't it? That's definitely how Hollywood would have done it." Dr. Shade laughed softly. "Good thing that 'gal' got on the stick, huh?"

Her mother shot Laurel a meaningful look.

Laurel just smiled. It was a smile of secret victory.

The girls had a wild pillow toss that night. Nightshade watched in astonishment, cringing at every pitch. But after the newness of the pillow toss wore off, he became more interested in the hair clips on top of the dresser. He began tapping them off the dresser and onto the floor, one at a time. He tapped each one with great precision, like a tiny golfer practicing his putt.

A sense of great urgency came over Laurel, out of nowhere. It rippled up and down her spine, amazing her with its strength. She grabbed a pillow and squeezed it to her chest as if her life depended on it.

"I want everything to be okay for the Holyfields!" She flopped straight backward onto her bed. "I guess that father didn't do anything terrible, at least not to the climbing tree. And I really really like Roberta, I like her so much. And the brother." Laurel was suddenly on the brink of tears. She swallowed hard. "That brother."

Jeanie looked thoughtful. "I understand," she said. "He just downloaded his way into your heart."

Laurel punched the pillow into a ball under her head and stared at the ceiling. If only she could read off some answers from up there on that bumpy surface.

Jeanie seemed to know her thoughts. "Do you still think he's some kind of cyberbeing?"

"I really don't know anymore," Laurel answered. "I was so convinced the father had messed with his brain somehow. But now I—I'm just not sure. I do know I want Roberta to have her real brother—whatever he is—and be happy. I hope all the bad stuff is over." Laurel sighed.

"Me too," Jeanie said quietly. "I'm hoping… to beat the band."

chapter 22

The next morning Laurel arrives at the Holyfields' very early. She had leapt out of bed and raced over as if every second mattered. Now that she's here, though, she doesn't know what to say. Strange to feel close to someone in some ways and still be so shy in others.

"Was it okay about the computer?" she asks Roberta. "Did your dad notice we left it on? Did he notice the other one was missing?" Her questions sound incredibly unimportant.

"He didn't notice anything." Roberta looks hesitant. Then, with a quick movement, she is hugging Laurel tightly and looking almost tearful. "Did you watch that meeting? Oh, Laurel, I can't even describe how I felt, it was so—so unbelievable!"

"You should feel good. I'm sure everything's going to be okay now."

"I do feel good! But last night I died about a thousand times. All those people who'd come to the meeting..."

"... and that chairman—he acted so grouchy, but I guess he was really okay..."

"... and my father refusing to go! He wasn't going to say a thing!"

"… but then good old Mr. Conti…"

"Good old you, you mean! You did it! You rescued my whole family…"

When most of the chattering is out of their systems, Roberta gives Laurel one of her earnest looks.

"You know what was so great? What made it so, like, perfect? Yesterday was my brother's birthday. And all things considered, it turned out pretty happy. I mean, just imagine if your father ended up in jail or something really horrible like that on your birthday!"

Laurel shudders, considering the horrors that might have been. "Yikes. Do you actually think they could have put your dad in jail?"

Almost immediately, this thought is eclipsed by a more urgent one. "Yesterday was your brother's birthday? So it was your birthday, too! Gosh." Laurel adds, more slowly: "I really wish you'd told me."

"It wasn't my birthday. I would have told you."

Laurel is dumbfounded. "But how could it not be your birthday, too? Aren't you guys twins?"

Roberta's mouth makes a twisty little smile. "No. We're not twins."

Laurel just stares. Roberta might as well have started speaking Arabic.

Very slowly, some corner of the confusion lifts. "So is your brother adopted or something?"

"We're both adopted, actually."

Too much has been happening. Laurel is getting almost light-headed trying to grasp it all.

She decides to put her thoughts together very slowly, one at a time. "Okay. So I guess that means… so you're not really, I mean, biologically…"

"Biologically, he's not really my brother."

Not really her brother?

He is not really her brother.

But now Roberta is jumping up, lunging toward the door, forehead wrinkled. "Laurel, you know that eight forty-five bell? Is that the first or the second bell?"

"The second bell. The late bell."

"Then we're going to be late," Roberta cries, and they run, breathless, to school.

As Laurel hurried through the halls to her classroom, an excited buzz seemed to follow her and to continue through the morning. Everyone in Mrs. Gombiner's class seemed to be grinning. There was more wildness and whispering than usual. *This feels familiar,* Laurel thought. *It feels like the day before a holiday.*

One thing was missing. David Holyfield's desk was empty.

In the middle of the morning he came into class, handing Mrs. Gombiner a note. As Laurel watched him settle into his seat, that yearning came up inside her—that yearning that now seemed to be a permanent ache between her lungs.

She thought of his birthday, just the day before. What would she have done if she'd known about it? And how would he have reacted? Why had he come in late? she wondered. She glanced with the usual guilty tingle at that lean jaw, that perfect wrist bone, that sublimely arching nose.

Something started drilling into Laurel's right shoulder blade. Collin. Laurel turned toward him, her stomach fluttering.

Apparently Collin was just feeling talkative. He motioned toward the Holyfield boy. "That dude reminds me of what Schmitt was talking about."

Laurel gave him a bewildered look. Then she just turned back around.

The insistent drilling on her shoulder blade started up again. Collin hadn't given up.

"You know, remember yesterday? When Schmitt was talking

about our brains and nervous systems and stuff and how they're like computers? With a kid like Holyfield, it's like they hook up, you know? He's on the keyboard so much it's almost like part of his hands. Know what I mean?"

"I think so," Laurel said in a hollow voice. "Kind of like the computer's part of him."

In a sense the computer was part of him.

When Laurel hurried out to meet Roberta on the playground after lunch, she saw several girls waiting at the low stone wall at the far end of the playground, at the place that was usually so empty. They were waiting for her and Roberta. Laurel headed toward them.

Shannon was the only girl in the usual spot near the playground equipment. She sat by herself on a swing. One leg was drawn up next to her. The other foot dangled, tracing one of the parallel ruts in the ground beneath the swing. She scribbled furiously in a notebook.

Laurel watched Shannon for a minute. Feelings of betrayal, then loss, swelled up and fell back again, like waves.

On Laurel's bulletin board at home was a snapshot of Shannon and Laurel at age seven. They were both grinning hugely, both missing their two front teeth. When exactly after that snapshot was taken, Laurel wondered, had Shannon stopped being her friend? Why had Laurel kept thinking they *were* friends—for so, so long? And what was Shannon feeling now?

"I wonder what Shannon is doing," she said out loud.

"I heard her saying she's going on some kind of trip tonight. She says she has a ton of stuff to do," Chrissie said. "She's going on a trip somewhere with that friend of hers, you know, that friend who goes to private school. I forget her name, something like Fairness or Justice or something."

"Justine," Laurel murmured. Just saying the name brought goose bumps to the back of her neck.

By now Roberta seemed to have met everyone. She'd been pulled into a group of three or four girls who were noisily developing a hip-hop dance routine.

Others were having quieter conversations. On one side Laurel overheard Sarah Teller, absently poking the blacktop with a stick, talking in low tones: "I mean, it's still a shame about the climbing tree, but you know, oh well…"

On Laurel's other side, a couple of voices groped and stumbled, giggling, trying to piece together the words to some song about a heart broken and words unspoken and a hopeless devotion.

And Laurel was listening to all these sounds, and yet somehow removed from them, too. She almost seemed to be floating above the playground, where she could hear the separate voices flow together and rise up into a strangely beautiful new sound, almost a hymn.

But she still wasn't at peace. She was still haunted by David Holyfield.

She cornered Computer Dave after school, right next to his cubby. He gave her that unreadable stare, almost as if he'd never seen her before, almost as if she weren't there. But she was resolved to face him. It was well past time.

She asked if he could walk home with her and Roberta, to talk about the Holyfields' computers. He answered yes.

On the way home he walked very fast, like he was trying to catch up with someone. Laurel had a hard time keeping pace.

"About your computer," she panted. "Roberta and I asked Mr. Schmitt to look at it and he said there was one huge file that had sort of splattered all over the hard drive. But it might be possible to reconstruct it with some disk-repair utility. He also wants to know if there's backup. I think this file might be big enough to store something huge… maybe… a human mind… so I need to know what kind of backup there might be."

Computer Dave hardly glanced at her. He kept up his break-
neck pace.

Laurel hurried after him. "So what kind of backup do you
have?"

Computer Dave looked at her again in that unseeing way, not
answering, barely pausing.

They were not quite at the Shades' house. Laurel stopped suddenly in her tracks. She felt rebellious.

Roberta, who had been gamely trying to keep up, now pulled
even with Laurel and touched her arm.

"Maybe *you* can get your brother to answer me," Laurel said to
her. It was only when Laurel heard the little quiver in her own
voice that she realized how angry she was.

Computer Dave started. He stopped and blinked. "I don't
understand what you're talking about," he said to Laurel. "And
why do you care about my computer?" Then he added, "Wait" in
a louder voice than usual.

"I can wait," Laurel said, puzzled.

"No," he said. "Jeanie." Then louder: "Jeanie, wait."

Laurel turned and saw Jeanie. Jeanie, it suddenly struck her, had
been walking her usual house and a half ahead of them. Now she
was trying ferociously to open the Shades' front door.

Laurel looked at her little sister, and then back at Computer
Dave. That strange look was in his eyes again. What *was* that look?
Curiosity? Amusement? Some kind of recognition? Whatever it
was, it was a feeling. It was something that, for the first time, made
his eyes look like real human eyes.

Everything went *click*. Laurel stood perfectly still for a minute,
feeling it all fall into place. Only then did she speak.

"You're not a computer anything." Her voice was surprisingly flat.
"You're just a boy. You're just a boy who… kind of likes my sister."

Saying the words made a sting of pain come up. But it was a

pain she could handle. It was like the sting of a scraped knee, not like an earache or anything, not like a real heartache. It was just a tiny hint of the pain she'd felt that day in the library when Shannon had called her a weirdo. Funny that the girl stuff would hurt more than the boy stuff.

Roberta had been standing silently at Laurel's elbow. As Laurel turned toward her now, Roberta seemed to be melting into the ground. "I can't even look at you," Roberta gasped. "I feel almost sick." She turned away to the side of the Shades' yard. She dropped to her knees on the grass. She threw her glasses down and covered her face with her hands.

Laurel came over and stood behind Roberta. She bent down and picked up the glasses. Then, awkwardly, she put her hand on Roberta's shoulder.

When Roberta started talking, every word was wooden, and separated from every other word. "I... am... ashamed. I got caught up in this... untrue thing. And I did not know how to get out of it."

"Stop it," Laurel said. "You didn't get caught up in it, I did."

"Those first couple times in the gym, when you first talked to me, you can never know how miserable I was. And you were so nice. And you were so intrigued by this thing about my brother. You had put all these pieces together about him being some kind of cyberbeing, and you were so fascinated, and I was, well, I guess I *wanted* you to be fascinated. I wanted *so much*... I wanted you to want to get to know me. I just played along with it. And then I didn't know how to get out of it. I lied to you."

"Oh, come on. I just convinced myself. I was on a mission. Funny, it already seems like so long ago. And so ridiculous. You must have thought I was a total idiot. Jeez, what was the matter with me?"

Laurel smacked her forehead. Oh man. What *had* been the matter with her? Of course boys didn't disappear into computers—

any more than kittens walked through walls. Funny how they both were drawn to Jeanie: the kitten and now the boy, too.

Laurel turned and studied her sister. Jeanie was rattling the doorknob crazily and making her sour face. A moment later she was staring at David Holyfield, looking very serious. And the next minute there was mischief in her eyes.

But what Laurel was seeing in her mind was the way Jeanie had looked that day in the library bathroom. Laurel was picturing that pointy, serious little face looking up at her, those large eyes glistening, that silent tear moving down one cheek. *"It's okay, Laurel.... Weirdo means something really good in Turbish."* A lump came up in Laurel's throat at the memory. Of all Jeanie's faces, that was the one that Laurel would never forget. She would not forget it ever, not even when she was really old.

By now Roberta was standing again. She put her glasses back on. She tucked some stray hairs behind her ears and sucked her breath in. "I just want to say one thing, Laurel. I never thought you were anything like an idiot. That first time we talked, I thought you were probably the most decent person I'd ever met. And now that I know you, well, now I'm *sure* you are."

Unexpectedly, Roberta grinned. She bent down and picked up two small rocks, one in each hand. "Hey, let's have a rock concert." She held one rock in front of her face and gave it a singing voice. "Rock, rock, baby, rock, rock! Rock, rock, baby, rock, rock!"

Laurel smiled and began looking for rocks of her own.

Snatches of conversation floated across the yard. Computer Dave appeared to be explaining the binary system to Jeanie. "So anything can be expressed in it, you see," they heard him pronounce in that Vulcan way of his.

"Big deal," they could hear Jeanie answer. "That's been true of Turbish for all these thousands of years."

Roberta and Laurel glanced at each other like two people who shared a private joke. Then Roberta asked softly, "Are you going to be okay with my brother? I know you really... *liked* him and everything."

"Oh yes. Oh jeez. It was just some weird thing. It's gone now." And it really was starting to feel like something in the past. Laurel began reflecting out loud. "I don't even understand what I felt. I don't think it was really even him I had a crush on. It was like... the *idea* of him. Or of some better version of him that maybe I could rescue from the computer."

"Well, you rescued me," Roberta said.

"Let me ask you something," Laurel said. "I mean... your brother doesn't really think of himself as a cyborg or a computer or anything, does he?"

Roberta chewed a thumbnail, thoughtful. "You know, my brother's different. I think he's a lot more comfortable with computers than he is with most people. Kind of like my dad. And another thing—it's strange because he's so incredibly *smart,* he's some kind of prodigy or something, but I think in a lot of ways he's very, very... well, young."

Roberta briefly inspected her thumb. "Now let me ask you something. Does your sister really think she's a television?"

"Jeanie doesn't think she's a television." Laurel paused and then had to laugh at how outrageous it all sounded. "Don't be ridiculous. She just thinks she has a television in her *head.* That's a very different thing." She cracked up.

"I guess those two have a lot in common," Roberta said. There was a short pause. Then they both said in the same breath: "Like screens."

And then the two of them were howling, clutching their sides, gasping, doubled over with the hilarity of this remark.

chapter 23

Sometime later, Laurel and Roberta sat on the steps of the Chestnut Knoll Racquet Club. They were waiting for Mrs. Shade to pick them up from tennis class.

Laurel gripped her tennis racquet between her knees. She kept trying to release it, then grip it with her knees again before it hit the ground. "Have you noticed how all the girls are saying 'holy smoke' now?" she said.

Roberta just rolled her eyes. Then she raised her eyebrows and bit her lower lip so that her teeth looked even more prominent than usual. It was Roberta's Thumper face, like Thumper in *Bambi*.

"Whatcha smilin' about?" Roberta asked in her Thumper voice.

"I don't know," said Laurel, suddenly aware that her grin was stretching her cheek muscles. "What about you? Why are *you* smiling so much?"

Just then the Shades' minivan pulled up. David and Jeanie sat in the far back. They were in their usual huddle, gesturing and widening their eyes in that intense way of theirs. Best buddies. They barely glanced up when Laurel and Roberta climbed into the car.

"Remind me to show you something later," Roberta whispered to Laurel.

★ ★ ★

When they got home, Roberta took her down to the trail. She showed her a new little tree. It had sprung up near the stump of the climbing tree.

This new tree looked distinctive, partly because its leaves were an unusual reddish color. *Born in blood* were the first words that flashed through Laurel's mind. But that was a thought she would never want to share with Roberta.

Roberta's own reaction was perfect. "You know, plants can understand things. They're supposed to even know what you're thinking. And they have something like memory, I read about it someplace."

She proposed that they write a song about how they got to be friends and then sing it to the little tree. She thought the tree might be able to store the song in its cells or the pattern of its wood grain or something. "And maybe in a hundred years two other girls will be best friends and really love this trail and wonder how such a special tree got here. And maybe the tree can kind of rustle that song to them."

Laurel squeezed Roberta's arm excitedly, and they began working on the song. They called it "The Ballad of Laurel and Roberta." Laurel was busy writing words for it in her head when she fell asleep that night.

It turned out she had a strange dream. She dreamed of a vacuum cleaner. It was somehow connected to her head, and she couldn't shut it off.

Groaning, she tried to shake the dream away. But nothing changed. The vacuum cleaner kept right on humming. She tried once more, harder this time, and finally managed to force her eyes open.

Nightshade was next to her. He was in a puffy ball right next to her face. He was kneading Laurel's shoulder, gently, and he was purring to beat the band.